The
Time-Traveling
Fashionista

AT THE PALACE OF MARIE ANTOINETTE

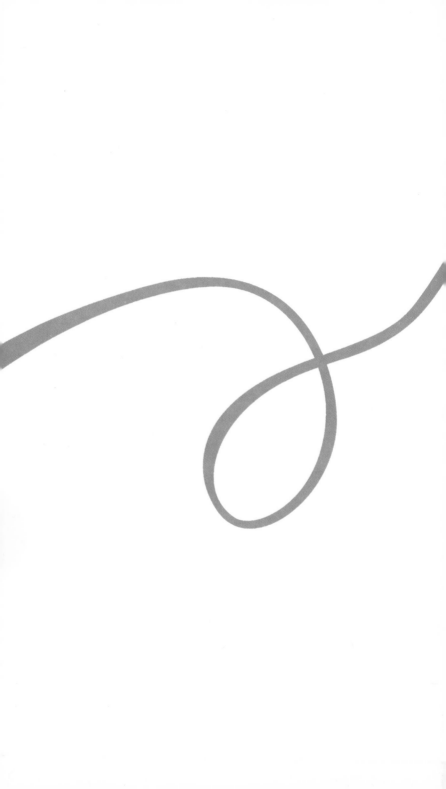

The Time-Traveling Fashionista

AT THE PALACE OF MARIE ANTOINETTE

a novel by

BIANCA TURETSKY

poppy

LITTLE, BROWN AND COMPANY
NEW YORK BOSTON

Also by Bianca Turetsky:

The Time-Traveling Fashionista On Board the Titanic

Poppy

Hachette Book Group
237 Park Avenue, New York, NY 10017
Visit our website at www.lb-kids.com

Poppy is an imprint of Little, Brown and Company.
The Poppy name and logo are trademarks of Hachette Book Group, Inc.

The publisher is not responsible for websites (or their content) that are not owned by the publisher.

First Edition: September 2012

Library of Congress Cataloging-in-Publication Data

Turetsky, Bianca.
  The time-traveling fashionista at the palace of Marie Antoinette : a novel / by Bianca Turetsky; [illustrations, Sandra Suy].— 1st ed.
     p. cm.— (The time-traveling fashionista ; 2)
  Summary: While seeking the perfect dress for her friend's birthday party, twelve-year-old Louise Lambert dons a vintage gown and finds herself with a young Marie Antoinette in eighteenth-century France, where, between cute commoner boys and glamorous trips to Paris, she finds that life in the palace is not all cake and couture.
  ISBN 978-0-316-10538-5
  [1. Space and time—Fiction. 2. Fashion—Fiction. 3. Magic—Fiction. 4. Marie Antoinette, Queen, consort of Louis XVI, King of France, 1755–1793—Childhood and youth—Fiction. 5. Courts and courtiers—Fiction. 6. France—History—Louis XVI, 1774-1793—Fiction. 7. Family life—Connecticut—Fiction. 8. Connecticut—Fiction.] I. Suy, Sandra, ill. II. Title.
  PZ7.T8385Tir 2012
  [Fic]—dc23   2012001553

10 9 8 7 6 5 4 3 2 1

SC

Book design by Alison Impey

Printed in China

For Cindy Eagan.
Love you, dahling.

"As far as I'm concerned, 'playing
dress-up' begins at the age of five
and never truly ends."

KATE SPADE,
American clothing and
handbag designer

CHAPTER 1

Louise is alone in the forest and it is dark. She knows that she has never been to these woods before; she is in new territory. The pounding of horses' hooves rumbles off in the background, and she stops walking and forces her eyes to adjust to the dim light. Out of the shadows, ten women in old-fashioned velvet cloaks clasped at the neck approach Louise and form a circle around her. She keeps still and alert, not wanting to show them how terrified she truly is. Inside she is shaking, but somewhere in her gut she knows that she is in charge, that these women are here to serve her. One of the cloaked figures approaches her and pulls off the red velvet cape Louise has protectively wrapped around her shoulders and lets it fall to the dirt. Louise hears the faint roar of thunder in the distance. A storm is coming soon.

They lead her into a makeshift wooden structure that is decorated inside like a fancy sitting room covered in royal blue brocade fabric, and Louise now feels as if she is playing a role in a very old ritual. A miniature white shih tzu is following her, trying to hide itself in the folds of her long crinoline skirts. Suddenly there is a frenzy of grabbing and pulling as the women tear off her clothing, ripping her beautiful ivory dress to rags, while she stands there helpless. *STOP!* Louise shrieks inside her head as a woman yanks the yellow satin ribbons from her hair. Another woman scoops up the yelping dog and quickly hurries out of the room before Louise can reach for it. The women take everything from her and toss the items carelessly onto the floor, even the delicate gold-and-ruby bracelet from her thin wrist. *Leave me alone! Somebody help me!* Louise blinks back hot, angry tears as her words get choked down inside her throat.

The matronly leader of the women then motions for the others to stop as she reverently hands Louise a new dress, a beautiful old-fashioned gown made of a fine powder blue silk that feels like liquid velvet, finer than anything she has ever owned before. Another lady gently pulls back Louise's hair with a long white silk ribbon, while yet another clasps a diamond-and-sapphire pendant on a sparkly silver chain around her neck. But despite her new luxurious adornments, Louise is still scared—alone in a strange place in the middle of the woods, far from all that is familiar to her. She knows that this has been planned and that her life is about to change forever. She is not the same girl anymore.

*   *   *

Louise Lambert bolted upright in bed. She was safe.

The somber sound of classical music filled her bedroom. How was it morning already? She rubbed her sleep-crusted eyes with the back of her hand and yawned. Sometimes her dream life was so active that Louise felt like she didn't even get a chance to sleep at all. She glanced over at her glowing clock radio: 7:17 AM. Time for another school day.

Louise liked waking up to a symphony; that way she could linger in her dream world for a little longer, like she wasn't abruptly grounded in her present reality quite yet. She could still be anywhere. She thought back to last night's nocturnal adventures and immediately felt like she was back in that blue brocade room, clinging to the ivory dress the women had taken off her that represented her old life so far away from home. But whose home, exactly? What old life? Those women in the woods were creepy; they wanted to turn her into someone she wasn't. And yet, in the end, it wasn't quite a nightmare, because they dressed her up in an even fancier gown and jewels. She could almost still feel the tickle of their silk-gloved hands softly brushing back her hair. But it left her with a majorly weird feeling. *Where did that scene come from?* Louise wondered as she propped herself up on her feather pillows. She pulled out her cherry red leather-bound journal and colored pencils from the top drawer of her bedside table and began drawing a rough sketch of the pale blue dress with its hoop skirt and fitted bodice before it completely evaporated from her memory. Maybe she could find something similar in her illustrated vintage dictionary, otherwise known as her fashion bible. She started flipping through the dog-eared pages of *Shopping for Vintage: The Definitive Guide to Fashion*, past the bright multicolored patterned Missonis and the outlandish Elsa Schiaparellis....

"Louise! *Breakfast!*" Her mom's shrill British voice pierced the quiet house. Jumping up from her warm, cozy, canopy bed, she changed out of her white-and-red-striped cotton pajamas and threw on a Mavi heather gray jersey dress (wishing it were an original by Diane von Furstenberg, the queen of the jersey wrap dress, from the seventies), a black lace Zac Posen for Target cardigan she had laid out the night before, and, as always, her neon pink Converse.

Automatically, she ripped off a page from her daily Virgo horoscope calendar, hoping to get some potential insight into her day. Louise didn't technically believe in astrological forecasts, but she also didn't used to believe in time travel, which she swore she had just done *for real* a few weeks ago, so now she wasn't sure what was real anymore. "Your values will be tested; hold on to what truly brings you happiness. The rest is just the icing on the cake." *Ummm, okay.* Her values were pretty much tested every day at Fairview Junior High, so that much was accurate. What would truly bring her happiness would be to stay home from school and

scour eBay and Etsy for the perfect pillbox hat or a one-of-a-kind vintage accessory. Although cake sounded pretty good right now—particularly when compared with the bland bowl of luke-warm oatmeal that was inevitably waiting for her downstairs.

"*Breakfast!*" reverberated throughout the huge drafty house. Her mom seemed to think the universe would come to a grinding halt if she missed her morning bowl of Quaker Oats.

"Be right down!" Louise shouted back, grabbing her antiquated Polaroid camera off the blond oak dresser. The bulky camera was a relic of her dad's from the eighties that she had discovered in a random steamer trunk in the basement. Louise had to special-order the expensive film online because the company didn't even produce it anymore, but to her it was worth it. She loved the dreamy and muted quality of the instant pictures that the camera noisily spit out. They looked like they could have been taken decades ago. And to Louise, that was a good thing. To put it simply, Louise was obsessed with all things vintage. From her mother, she had inherited a love of classic films, but, unlike her mom, she also developed an obsession with fashion from those bygone eras. Her sizable walk-in closet was quickly filling up with her ever-expanding collection of thrift-store finds.

She pointed the camera down at herself and smiled—a hesitating smile, the tight-lipped grin of a girl with a mouth crammed full of silver braces—and snapped a picture. It was her daily ritual that she'd started several months ago on her twelfth birthday, a visual diary that one day she planned to make into a book. She labeled the gray underdeveloped photo *June 5* with a black ballpoint pen and stashed it in her sock drawer just as the cloudy film was beginning to come into focus.

Louise caught a glimpse of the teal-colored Traveling Fashionista invitation that was partially hidden underneath her navy blue ribbed wool tights and reread the now familiar information with a tickling, nervous excitement.

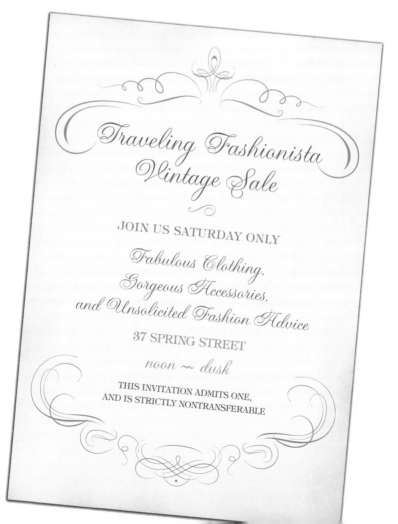

Traveling Fashionista Vintage Sale

JOIN US SATURDAY ONLY

Fabulous Clothing, Gorgeous Accessories, and Unsolicited Fashion Advice

37 SPRING STREET

noon ~ dusk

THIS INVITATION ADMITS ONE, AND IS STRICTLY NONTRANSFERABLE

Louise knew from her daily photographs that on the outside she looked pretty much like she did before she went to the initial Traveling Fashionista Vintage Sale: same flat chest, frizzy brown pulled-back hair, annoying braces. But she also felt as if something inside her had shifted.

The first invitation, printed on thick purple stationery, mysteriously arrived unaddressed and with no postage on an otherwise typical April afternoon. She showed up at the unfamiliar Chapel Street location, not sure of what to expect, as none of her friends had received a similar invitation. But as soon as Louise walked into the curious shop, she was bedazzled by the endless selection of clothing, shoes, and accessories from every era and vintage designer she idolized. The cluttered store was run by two colorfully eccentric salesladies, Marla and Glenda, who reluctantly let her try on the most incredible pink shimmery evening gown, which ended up fitting her perfectly. Perhaps a bit *too* perfectly, as before she knew it, Louise found herself actually waking up in the life of a Miss Alice Baxter, the previous owner of the dress, on board a ship a hundred years ago. She also happened to be Louise's great-aunt! Oh, and the other minor detail was that the ship happened to be…the *Titanic*. What had started out as a search for the perfect dress for Fairview Junior High's semiformal turned into something much more mind-blowing and insanely adventurous.

It was like her life had finally decided to wake up and start getting good. For some reason that she had yet to fully comprehend, Louise had been the one chosen to receive these invitations. Maybe hers was the kind of life where adventurous things actually happened. Like all of her twelve years of waiting wasn't for nothing. According to the handwritten letter she later received from Marla and Glenda, she was a Fashionista now. She'd found the invitation to the second sale with this note on her bedside table.

"Last warning, Louise Lambert!"

She could get lost in these memories and daydreams for hours, but at this particular moment, Louise still needed to catch the bus. She grabbed her faded purple backpack and sprinted down the curved and creaky main staircase to force down another torturously balanced meal.

CHAPTER 2

"Thirteen is, like, a big deal. I mean, I'm officially a teenager," Brooke Patterson announced while applying strawberry-scented lip gloss to her already perfect red pout in the locker mirror. "Twelve always felt kind of babyish. No offense, Louise."

"None taken. Anyway, I think I kind of like babyish. I'm not ready to give up the Barbie Dream House yet." Louise was kidding. Sort of. "Of course, you probably won't want to hang out with me this summer while you're thirteen and I'm still an infantile twelve," she said, twirling a flyaway strand of hair that had escaped her auburn brown ponytail.

Louise anxiously looked over at her friend, who was wearing a heather gray scoop-neck T-shirt with a little Abercrombie moose embroidered on the pocket, a dark denim miniskirt, black leggings, and camel-colored Uggs (even though it was almost seventy degrees outside). The overcrowded hall was a noisy cacophony of slamming lockers, yelling teachers, and squeaky rubber-soled sneakers skidding across the swamp green linoleum floor.

She didn't want her best friend to grow up without her, and yet, without fail, each year since they were babies, Brooke did just that. At least for the three months until Louise would turn thirteen as well. Louise sometimes did still play with her old Barbies, which she kept hidden in the back of her walk-in closet in a beaten-up, nondescript black steamer trunk that used to belong to her mom. But she played with them in a more mature way now, like they solved mysteries and had Barbie kisses.

"Whatever, it's just a number," Brooke sighed, so clearly not believing that.

"Right," Louise agreed. "Besides, thirteen is unlucky. Elevators don't even stop there. So if your life were like a building, you would still be stuck at twelve like me. Or already at fourteen."

"An elevator? What are you talking about, Lou?" Brooke asked, giving her mirror image one last glossy pucker. "Are you jealous?"

"Yes," Louise admitted. They both laughed.

"Anyway, my party has to be monumental. Historic. It has to go down in the Fairview Junior High School history books as the most amazing thirteenth birthday party. Ever."

"You should have a theme party!" Louise cried suddenly, then looked down at her pink Converse, wondering if that was a tad childish of a suggestion. Like something only a twelve-year-old would think of?

"Love it!" Brooke squealed.

"It can be a fancy dress-up party." Louise grinned. "You can write on the invitations that the girls have to wear dresses and boys won't be allowed in without a suit and tie. Or at least the tie part."

"Perfect! Like prom, but not."

"Exactly!" Louise loved coming up with ideas like this.

"Maybe you can get something to wear at the next Fashionista Sale?" Brooke asked hesitantly.

"Maybe..."

Ever since Louise's adventure as Miss Baxter on the *Titanic*, her best friend, who had never bought anything not in a mall or department store, had suddenly developed an interest in her vintage collection. Louise was pretty sure it was because her friend thought she had gone off the deep end and wanted to keep an eye on her sanity. Brooke, not surprisingly, didn't exactly believe Louise's completely crazy–sounding story of how she had spent a few amazing days on board the infamous ship experiencing the life of her great-aunt Alice, a wildly rich and beautiful actress. Brooke had gone with her to the sale, and to her it just seemed like Louise had passed out with a high fever. Even when she showed her friend the old grainy newspaper photograph she found online taken on the A Deck of the White Star Line, aka the *Titanic*, dated April 12, 1912, Brooke still didn't take her seriously. Louise had to admit the tiny image was pixelated and blurry, but she knew deep down that it was undeniably herself in that picture standing alongside Jacob and Madeleine Astor even though there was no rational way to explain any of it. At least she had this proof for herself. She knew she wasn't crazy. *Right?*

After Brooke's skeptical reaction, Louise didn't show anyone else that photo, not even her parents. They probably wouldn't believe her anyway, and if they did, she didn't want to spend the rest of her seventh-grade school year hooked up to electrodes and being tested as a time-traveling science experiment in a lab somewhere. Instinctively, she knew that her experience with the two witchy stylists she'd met at the magical Fashionista Vintage Sale was something special she should keep protected. Especially if she wanted to go back to the second sale—which she knew she did, considering that Marla and Glenda possessed the most amazing collection of designer vintage clothing Louise had ever seen. Of course, she was also really excited at the prospect of time-traveling again.

"We'll see when or if I get another invitation," Louise

eventually replied, crossing her fingers behind her back because this wasn't exactly true. She had found the invitation to the next sale on her bedside table the same night she woke up from the supposed hallucinations brought on by a severe bout of food poisoning from the rancid crab dip Marla had given her at the Fashionista Sale. Or at least that's how her parents rationalized the whole thing. She was somewhat nervous to go back a second time, but the possibility of something actually happening again in her otherwise mundane existence (or of finding an original Vivienne Westwood kilt, Balenciaga flamenco-style dress, or something equally fabulous and rare) made those butterflies a moot point.

Louise realized this was the first secret she had deliberately kept from Brooke, and it made her feel both uncomfortable and a little special at the same time. It was the first thing that was only hers. She sort of wanted to keep it that way at least for a little while. Brooke honestly didn't care that much about vintage fashion. Also, for once, *Louise* was the one who had been chosen.

"Okay, cool," Brooke replied, running her pink manicured fingers through her wavy golden locks. Yes, she had golden locks.

Usually it was Brooke who was the Chosen One. She was a straight-A student, involved in practically every extracurricular activity Fairview offered, except for the ones like math league and chess club, and unassumingly pretty in a way that made it impossible for guys, girls, teachers, parents, and everyone else, for that matter, *not* to like her. With her clear blue eyes and long, wavy, sun-streaked blonde hair (which miraculously glowed even in the dead of a Connecticut winter), Brooke had never been subjected to what Louise's mom gently called "an awkward phase"—which in Louise's case was obviously a euphemism for "really ugly unfortunate few years."

Louise, on the other hand, felt like she was indeterminably stuck in hers. No matter how many different Frizz-Away conditioners and serums she put in her hair, they were no match for the chlorine that fried her auburn curls for two hours every day during Coach Murphy's swim practices. She had a feeling those grueling workouts also contributed to the fact that her double-A-cup bra was still a little baggy and her period, which she desperately wanted for no other reason than to prove that she was a normal almost-thirteen-year-old girl, had yet to arrive. On top of all that, she still had another three months, two weeks, and six days before her braces came off. Not that she was counting or anything.

"Okay, I'm going to be late for gym," Brooke said as the warning bell rang, and she slammed her locker shut. Louise smiled; typical that her best friend would spend fifteen minutes meticulously fixing her hair and applying lip gloss before rushing off to play dodgeball. "See you on the bus!"

"Don't remind me." Louise groaned. The bus ride was currently the bane of her existence because this year Billy Robertson had made it his job to annoy her on the drive to and from school, mostly about whatever vintage piece she was wearing that day. He thought her unique style was "old" and "ratty." In Brooke's expert opinion, that was his way of flirting; in Louise's limited experience, it was just embarrassing.

Today in particular, she wasn't feeling too hot. While eating a forbidden Twix bar at lunch, all the more delicious now that its chocolate-and-caramelly goodness was banned by her orthodontist, Louise had felt the metal wire on her upper left brace snap. Her mouth was currently of chipmunk proportions, swollen and crammed full of wax, until she could make her emergency appointment after school.

So it was pretty much a given that she would run into Todd Berkowitz at that moment. Something peculiar had happened since she came back from being Miss Baxter. She kind of . . . well, cared. Todd had not exactly been transformed from a shaggy-haired frog into a skateboard-riding, baggy-pants-wearing prince, but Louise's consciousness had shifted. She hated to admit it, even to herself, but she now wanted to look good if he was around. Louise had spent the first half of middle school literally running away from him. It took a voyage back to 1912 and meeting a totally hot, rich creep named Benjamin Guggenheim for her to realize that Todd may not have been the man of her dreams, but he was actually pretty cool.

She thought back to slow dancing with him at the semiformal shortly after she got back from her *Titanic* adventure. At first, she had been scared to put on the Lucile dress again, afraid she would open her eyes and find herself back on the ship, but all was okay. In some way it must have already served its purpose. She and Todd hadn't really been dancing, just kind of swaying to the music and shuffling their feet a little. Without realizing it until later, Louise had pretty much held her breath through the entire three-minute song. She'd then had to discreetly wipe her sweaty hands on the flowing silk skirt of the pink vintage Lucile dress when she and Todd had awkwardly unhooked themselves after the DJ abruptly transitioned into a Beyoncé song. Todd Berkowitz had turned into someone who could make her nervous! It was infuriating and unexpected.

Even though they technically went to the dance together because Todd had asked her earlier that week, Louise spent most of the night hanging out by the punch bowl with Brooke and some other girls in their grade who went alone or had also abandoned their dates, because that was still more fun. Louise and Todd had supposedly gone to the dance as a couple, but that didn't stop Todd from slow dancing with Tiff Freedman

21

while Louise was helping herself to another glass of overly sweetened fruit punch. She had assumed going to the dance with someone meant *not* slow dancing with other girls. Apparently, she'd been wrong.

Since that night, she and Todd had hung out a bit more in school, but it wasn't like in the old movies Louise watched, when a boy would give you his letter jacket or class ring and then you and everyone else would *know* that things were different. They were kind of just a little different.

The sound of Todd's snorting laughter in the hallway snapped her back to reality. Louise and her swollen cheek hid behind her flimsy beige metal locker door as he walked by with his eyes partially covered by his floppy auburn hair, wearing his gray hooded sweatshirt and New Balance sneakers, laughing and joking around with Tiff Freedman. He held his beaten-up skateboard in one hand and some textbooks in the other. *Tiff's books?*

Tiff Freedman was a transfer student from California who wore peasant blouses and bell-bottom jeans with Birkenstocks every day. Even in the winter, but with wool socks. She probably loved camping and jam bands, and she had long, straight, frizz-free honey blonde hair that, unlike Louise's overfried split ends, had never seen the hot end of a straightening iron. She was undeniably, naturally beautiful. Like a modern-day Joni Mitchell, one of Louise's mother's favorite folksingers from the seventies. In Louise's mind, Tiff was everything she wasn't, and in this moment she was pretty unhappy about it.

Louise grabbed her own brown-paper-bag-covered math book, which was now almost completely filled with colored-pencil fashion sketches, and hastily shoved it into her beat-up purple backpack before rushing off in the other direction to her last class.

CHAPTER 3

When her father was home in time for dinner, she knew
something was wrong. Her mother was always anxious, but
Louise sensed that tonight Mrs. Lambert was particularly
nervous, banging around the cavernous kitchen trying to get
her bland, boiled, overcooked concoction on the table. She
seemed incredibly flustered to see Mr. Lambert home so early.
The Lamberts' Tudor-style home was a great big sprawling
and creaky house much too large for a family of three. But it
was the perfect place for a game of hide-and-seek, as the extra
bedrooms and the back staircase (which at one point was probably used by the servants) made for plenty of excellent hiding
spots. Most of Louise's playdates when she was younger ended
up turning into some version of hide-and-seek.

"Set the table, dahling. Your father is home," Mrs. Lambert
ordered, stating the obvious. Louise pulled three white Wedg-
wood china plates out of the buffet and placed them carefully

on one corner of the long mahogany dining room table. Her father always worked late hours at his law firm in New York City. The times he did make it home early, he would call from Grand Central Terminal before he got on the Metro-North commuter train, and they would wait for him and go out for Thai food, his and Louise's favorite. He was as much a fan of his wife's cooking as Louise was, meaning: not at all. Mrs. Lambert grew up in England with maids, nannies, and a private cook and therefore never had to learn how to turn on the stove; she was infamous for turning even the most basic recipe into an unrecognizable and inedible concoction.

"Hi, chicken," Mr. Lambert greeted his daughter, absent-mindedly placing a kiss on the top of her damp, frizzy head. "I'll be down in a minute."

Louise looked at him curiously—same wire-rimmed glasses, cropped gray hair, Brooks Brothers suit—and tried to figure out what was different as she set up the silverware, forks on the left, knives and spoons on the right.

Her mom, with her perfectly coiffed ash blonde hair and cream-colored cashmere sweater set, precariously carried a steaming casserole dish of something (the smell didn't help decode that mystery) to the table in her right hand, a glass of white wine in her left hand. She rarely drank during the week, so this was either a special occasion or her parents were about to drop a big bombshell on her. Like they were getting divorced or moving to Australia? Louise said a quick silent prayer for the second option.

Her dad walked back into the Venetian red formal dining room, gloomily lined with ornately framed oil portraits of their family's dusty ancestors, including an old painting of her great-aunt Alice Baxter, who was completely unrecognizable from the gorgeous young woman Louise had embodied on the *Titanic*. Her dad was wearing an old gray-and-purple NYU T-shirt (since when were they allowed to dress *down* for dinner?) and carrying a glass tumbler of golden liquid clinking with ice.

"Let's get this out of the way," Mr. Lambert announced, taking a large gulp of his cocktail. "There were layoffs today; the firm is now about half as big as it was yesterday. And let's just say I'll be seeing my two favorite girls a lot more this summer."

"Oh, dear," Mrs. Lambert replied, twisting the pearls around her neck so tautly Louise thought they would break and ricochet all over the dining room. "Well, I suppose you'll simply find a new job, right, dahling?" she asked in her very drawn-out English accent, shakily sitting down in her high-back mahogany chair.

"If you can point me to a firm that's actually taking on lawyers in this economy, then I will gladly show up with my briefcase and résumé. But until then I'm looking forward to a little vacation. So what's for dinner?" he asked in a tone that seemed to announce this particular conversation was over.

Mrs. Lambert delicately placed her linen napkin on her lap. "But we need to repair the roof, and we just bought the new Volvo...."

"Not now, please, dear. Well, what do we have here? Tuna noodle surprise? Another English classic!" Louise's father exchanged a secret bemused look with his daughter as he scooped out a lump of grayish noodles that landed on his plate with a surprising thunk. His wife instinctively passed him a bottle of malt vinegar, her go-to condiment for absolutely everything. "You know what? Maybe I'll take a cooking class in my downtime. I can be Mr. Mom." Mrs. Lambert's eyes widened in horror.

"Awesome!" Louise exclaimed. She felt bad for her dad but also kind of excited that she would finally get some quality time with him and, quite possibly, a decent meal out of this situation. They'd never had a problem with money before. Her parents must have some savings, right?

"What about Mr. Patterson?" she asked, remembering that Brooke's dad worked for the same firm. "Was he laid off, too?"

"No, he's part of the other half," her dad replied, a flicker of emotion crossing his otherwise calm face. "The dark side," he added with a fake wicked cackle. Louise laughed as she poked around at the strange gelatinous noodles in front of her, but inside she was also starting to feel a little nervous about this change that had suddenly descended on their family. She turned toward her mom for some reassurance that they would be fine. Mrs. Lambert was looking straight ahead into the distance; it seemed as though her worries had already carried her a million miles away.

CHAPTER 4

"What's this?" Brooke asked the next day after school, holding out a colorful jewel-toned silk scarf, Louise's latest Salvation Army purchase, between her fingertips as though it were contagious. As much as she was trying to feign an interest in Louise's vintage collection, it was *so* clearly not in her nature. Brooke must have realized that in some small way her best friend had a passion that they didn't share together.

"It's great, no? Like sixties Pucci or something? I bought it for three dollars last week," Louise gushed, proud of her find. Generally, at the two local thrift stores, otherwise known as Goodwill and Salvation Army, the only labels you were likely to come across were preppy mom ones like Ann Taylor and Talbots. This time she totally lucked out.

"It's…interesting," Brooke finally said, carelessly tossing it over the back of Louise's mahogany rolling desk chair. Her giant orange goldfish, Marlon, swam in lazy circles around his bowl on top of her desk. The furniture in her room was a mismatch of antiques and Ikea, with a newly acquired six-foot-tall bookcase already overflowing with classic novels like *Little Women* and *A Wrinkle in Time*, as well as a bunch of fashion books she'd read but wasn't ready to give away yet. Louise's clothing was strewn inside out on most available surfaces. It took her a few tries to figure out what she was going to wear the next day, and often the pieces that didn't make the cut wound up on the furniture or Oriental rug.

"Thanks, that *almost* sounds like a compliment," Louise teased as she watched Brooke attempt to check herself out in the full-length mirror, which was challenging, as most of the reflective surface was covered in glossy magazine tear-outs and black-and-white prints of Katharine Hepburn, Cary Grant, and other black-and-white-movie Hollywood stars of bygone eras.

Sometimes Louise wished she had someone to talk to about her vintage obsession, someone else who worshipped at the altar of Christian Dior and Yves Saint Laurent. Someone who knew that Emilio Pucci was an Italian fashion designer who created colorful, geometric-patterned dresses and scarves rather than being a breed of lapdog or something.

Unfortunately the likelihood of finding someone at her suburban middle school with an appreciation for vintage designers was about as probable as finding Justin Bieber in her eighth-period English lit class. Totally not going to happen in this universe. At least she had discovered some good blogs about vintage and fashion that she checked religiously, like *What I Wore* and *Style Rookie*, so Louise didn't feel totally alone. There were other girls like her out there somewhere....

Brooke sat down at the edge of the canopy bed. "I'm sorry to hear about your dad," she said quietly in that tone reserved for really awful things like when Brooke told her she spotted Todd and Tiff slow dancing at the semiformal. Like if she didn't say it in a loud voice it wouldn't hurt so much. This only resulted in Louise thinking she had misheard, so Brooke had to deliver the devastating blow three times before her best friend finally got the message. And yes, it still hurt. A lot.

"Thanks," Louise answered defensively. She was stretched out across her full-size bed, flipping through the latest issue of *Teen Vogue*. "But he's not dead, just temporarily unemployed. He'll find another job." The magazine had recently started running a new column following one girl on a cross-country road trip as she stopped at every thrift store she passed and did a photo shoot in her new/old outfits. Louise would give anything to be on a similar odyssey. Would the magazine ever believe she had traveled on the *Titanic* and had an old black-and-white photo on her computer as proof?

"Of course," Brooke replied quickly, playing with a loose thread on Louise's patchwork quilt. "I just meant that it sucks to lose your job in this economy, but he's one of the best lawyers in the tristate area. I'm sure he'll find a new firm." Brooke sounded like she was repeating something her parents must have said at dinner the night before. Was everyone talking about her family now? Like they were a charity case? God, her mother would be mortified.

"Anyway, aren't you so excited for the Paris trip?" Brooke asked cheerfully, trying to change the subject. Every June, the seventh-grade AP French class went on a trip to France led by their overly enthusiastic French teacher, Madame Truffant. How she had managed to persuade the school board to let her escort a group of undersupervised, overstimulated seventh graders with a less-than-firm grasp on basic French vocab across the Atlantic Ocean was anyone's guess. But it was by far the highlight of the school year and the main reason French class was way more popular at their school than Spanish or, God forbid, Latin.

"I don't know if I'm even going anymore. We're supposed to have a family meeting about it tonight," Louise replied.

When you're an only child and your parents call for a "family meeting," then you know something is up in a bad way. The chances of them meeting to talk about how much fun Louise would have in France were pretty much nonexistent.

"Lou, you have to go. For my sake. And what about Todd? You can't have him crossing international borders alone with Tiff!" Brooke trilled, jumping up from the bed. On the bus ride home, Louise had completely filled her in on what she had seen that afternoon in the hallway. This was a disturbing development, particularly after Tiff had been slow dancing and flirting with Todd at the semiformal even though she must have known that Louise and Todd were…well, she wasn't exactly sure what they were, so she definitely didn't need any competition at this point. For now, Tiff Freedman was the enemy.

"Don't you think I know that?" Louise asked dramatically. Paris was the city she had been dreaming of since she saw her first Hermès Birkin bag in the pages of her mother's British *Vogue*. Her French was *pas mal* thanks to endless hours of foreign films she watched trying to emulate the styles of Brigitte Bardot and Anna Karina, two of her favorite French actresses from the sixties. *Très chic.*

But now, thanks to the recession, her chances of shopping in the City of Light were slim to nonexistent. The universe and the national Treasury were obviously conspiring against her.

"Good luck. I've got to get home for dinner, but remember you *have* to go to Paris," Brooke repeated as if Louise had a choice in the matter. "Call me after and tell me everything."

"I will," Louise sighed, getting up and wrapping her new faux-Pucci scarf around her head like an exotic turban. She gave her best friend two air kisses. That's how they said goodbye in foreign countries, or at least in foreign films.

CHAPTER 5

The Lambert family meetings were held in the formal living room, a place that Louise typically was not even allowed to step foot in because of the pristine ivory Belgian linen upholstery, invaluable antique vases, and decorative glass bowls displayed on every available surface. It was like a weird museum that no one visited except for the times when her parents hosted cocktail parties for her father's law firm. She guessed that wouldn't be happening anymore.

Louise had been forced to attend these meetings twice before: once when her grandfather died, and once when her gray cat, Bogart (named after Humphrey Bogart, who starred in one of her and her mom's favorite classic films, *Casablanca*, from the forties), got run over by a mail truck. It was no wonder that her stomach sank down to her Converse sneakers when another was scheduled. Why couldn't they just break the bad news at breakfast like normal parents instead of having her anticipate it all day long? They took this meeting thing way too seriously. She was surprised *not* to see her mother in her neutral-toned cashmere sweater set and pearls, perched on the edge of her overstuffed armchair with a yellow legal notepad recording the minutes. *Seven thirty PM. Louise Lambert promptly enters the living room.*

"You don't have enough money to send me to Paris with the class," Louise predicted as she plopped down on the uncomfortable white sofa, defiantly eating a half-melted bowl of Ben & Jerry's New York Super Fudge Chunk ice cream. "Let's get this out of the way."

Her parents were caught off guard—she seemed to have ruined their scripted performance. Her mother eyed the soupy brown bowl with trepidation. Louise half expected her to excuse herself to grab a preemptive bottle of club soda.

"Ummm, yes. Unfortunately that appears to be the case," her father stuttered, running his hand through his cropped silver hair. "You know we've always been supportive of your extracurricular activities, but in all honesty, we can't afford the additional expense, thanks to Gladstone, Braden LLP." He raised his glass tumbler in a sarcastic gesture and took a swig of his now ever-present cocktail.

"But, dahling, once we get back on our feet, we'll take a nice family trip to Europe," her mother added, quickly scooting a coaster under Mr. Lambert's glass before he could set it unprotected on the oak side table and leave a water mark. "Won't that be fun?"

Did they not see how vastly different those two options were?

"Great," Louise said dully. "Can I be excused now?"

"I hope you understand. I'm sorry, chicken." Her father looked genuinely pained as he took off his square wire-rimmed glasses and rubbed his eyes. "I really am."

"I know." Louise nodded, her face getting hot. And she did. She didn't want to seem like a spoiled only child, but she also couldn't help but think this was entirely unfair. While the rest of her class was in Paris bonding, laughing, and creating a million inside jokes that "you just had to be there for," she would be alone, sitting in her bedroom bored out of her mind, obsessing over the freshly baked croissants she wasn't eating. The more she thought about it, the bigger the lump in her throat got.

"But at least we still have our good looks," her father joked. Louise didn't crack a smile. *Who exactly was he referring to?* she wondered angrily, tucking a flyaway frizzy hair behind her ear.

She slammed her half-eaten bowl on the glass coffee table with a clatter and ran out of the room before she started crying. She needed to talk to her best friend.

*   *   *

"I'm not going," Louise sobbed into her oversized eighties red lip phone, angrily pacing her room as far as the tangled cord would allow without the jack being yanked out of the wall.

"No!" Brooke screamed. Louise pulled the phone away from her ear. *Ouch.* She wished she had speakerphone on this old thing.

"I know. They suggested we take a family trip to Europe when my dad gets another job." She paused, still not able to comprehend how clueless parents could be sometimes.

"*No!*" Brooke screamed again, directly into Louise's brain. "That is so unfair."

"That's what I said," Louise confirmed glumly. They were both quiet for a moment, letting the bad news sink in. "And all this time, I could have been taking Spanish," she added, thinking of the interminable hours she slaved over her French irregular verbs and vocabulary. For nothing.

"Well, I guess it could be worse," her friend reasoned diplomatically. "I mean, at least you won't have to deal with a seven-hour plane ride with Billy Robertson kicking the back of your seat."

"I guess," Louise mumbled. Somehow that was small consolation. She had actually been looking forward to the seven-hour flight—it meant she was actually going somewhere. "Well, try not to have too much fun without me."

There was a long pause. That was all there was to say. For once, Brooke was speechless.

CHAPTER 6

"Attention, class," Miss Morris gasped, as if those could very well be her last words ever. "Today we are going to take a trip to France."

Louise looked around her quiet history classroom filled with blank faces. If it was medically feasible to sleep with your eyes open, then 75 percent of this class was definitely getting some quality REM time right now. Miss Morris was quite possibly the only person on the planet who could offer up a trip to France and get absolutely no reaction whatsoever. Not even a raised eyebrow. She had probably planned this lesson in conjunction with Madame Truffant's field trip, but this was definitely not the expedition abroad that Louise had been wishing for.

The white-haired history teacher wasn't exactly dressed for a voyage to Europe, Louise noticed, eyeing her navy blue boiled-wool jacket and knee-length pencil skirt. A slight variation on the uncomfortable-looking suit she wore every day, regardless of the season...or decade. Miss Morris was definitely not influenced by current fashion trends, and, unfortunately for Louise, she was probably the only other person at Fairview Junior High who wore vintage, just not in a good way.

Louise glanced down at her blank loose-leaf notebook page and began to draw an old-fashioned high-heeled shoe with a big diamond buckle. It looked...French? She wasn't sure; she would have to research that in her vintage fashion book when she got home.

"If you think we are in dire economic straits now..." Miss Morris said, pausing to erase the remnants of yesterday's notes off the chalkboard. She was practically the only teacher in the whole school who refused to embrace the whiteboard and insisted on writing everything out on the green chalkboard in her tiny, practically illegible script.

Yes, I do, Louise thought over the deafening sound of the second hand creeping its way around the institutional clock.

Click, click, click.

"Then you clearly haven't read your homework about the French Revolution," her teacher continued drily. *Oops!* Louise was usually totally on top of her assignments, but last night she had been a little...distracted. She had stayed up until after midnight obsessively looking at pictures of Paris online—

the Eiffel Tower, the Louvre, the Tuileries Gardens, the Champs-Elysées—since her computer screen was as close to France as she was going to get at this point.

"Throughout the country, the French people of the eighteenth century were plagued with a nationwide famine and malnutrition. There was an exorbitantly high national debt, only made worse by an unfair system of taxation, which heavily penalized those who could afford it the least. The common working people were struggling to survive, while the royal monarchy lived a lavish and luxurious lifestyle behind their gilded palace doors."

Louise didn't want to think about some revolution that happened to other people hundreds of years ago. She couldn't stop thinking about her own dire economic situation that was happening right now. What else was going to change now that her dad wasn't working? So far she was going to miss the class trip. Just repeating those words in her head made her eyes hot and stingy. She was missing the first opportunity that seemed full of potential for amazing things to happen in her actual life. She looked around the room and saw her nemesis, Billy, lying on his open textbook with his eyes closed, drooling. In the classrooms of Fairview, Connecticut, the potential for amazing things happening seemed totally nonexistent.

"In 1789, seven thousand armed working-class women

marched to Versailles carrying cannons to demand that the king and queen address their concerns about the bread shortages. The queen of France, Marie Antoinette, and her family were exiled from their home at Versailles in the middle of the night in fear for their lives. The royal family was later put on trial and imprisoned under harsh conditions. Ultimately, Marie Antoinette was executed by guillotine in front of a bloodthirsty mob. Her severed head was held up high above for all in the screaming crowd to see," Miss Morris continued in her same flat monotone. *Say what?* Louise snuck a look around to see if anyone else in the class was catching this. She saw a few surprised faces of her previously sleepy classmates start to perk up.

"This young queen, who originally hailed from Austria and whose marriage to King Louis XVI had been used by her mother as a strategic negotiating tool with France, had now become the symbol of the excess and frivolity of the doomed French monarchy. Her murderers were generous enough not to parade her bloodied head through the streets of Paris on a spike, as they did to her dear friend the Princesse de Lamballe. The poor Princesse de Lamballe's detached head was first taken to a hairdresser, ensuring that everyone, particularly Marie Antoinette, would recognize her." Now all eyes were facing the front of the classroom, watching their elderly teacher, who looked even tinier standing behind her large oak teacher's desk, lecture matter-of-factly about the most gruesome murders Louise had ever heard of. Even Billy Robertson had wiped the drool from the side of his mouth and was eagerly leaning forward, not wanting to miss a word.

"The former queen of France was thrown into an unmarked grave, her once beautiful face now separated from her delicate slim torso, alongside her husband, Louis XVI, who was killed in the same cruel manner a few months prior." Louise's mouth dropped open in shock. Way gross.

BRIIIIINGGGG. The bell rang and no one moved. Miss Morris had finally grabbed their attention.

CHAPTER 7

"Do you know how long I've waited to go on this trip to Paris?" Louise asked, placing a low-fat strawberry Stonyfield Farm yogurt on her otherwise empty lunch tray. "Since sixth grade," she answered before Brooke had a chance to respond.

"Diet much?" Brooke asked her with a raised eyebrow as she helped herself to some sweet-potato fries, which looked as though they had been baking under the infrared heat lamp for eons. They had previously concluded that sweet-potato fries were the perfect combination of vitamins and fast food. "And Louise, no offense, but sixth grade was last year."

"Brooke, I'm depressed. I'm not supposed to be eating."

Brooke rolled her eyes and grabbed an extra helping for Louise. "What inane fashion magazine told you that ridiculousness? Are you reading old issues of *Cosmo* again?" she joked.

The overcrowded lunchroom, which also doubled as an

auditorium during nonlunch hours, was bustling and buzzing with pent-up energy. It was hard to hear her best friend talk, and she was standing right next to her. The overlit room was configured with the maximum number of both long and round tables, arranged in a way that made walking from one side to the other feel like navigating a labyrinth. A blue-and-gold banner of Ozzie the Otter, the school mascot, hung above the doorway, reminding everyone to recycle their milk cartons. Louise caught Todd and Tiff laughing across the crowded room, standing against the far wall in the first hot-lunch line together. When Tiff tossed her straight blonde hair flirtatiously over her shoulder, Louise was forced to look away. Could she be more obvious? Louise thought that she and Todd had had a good time at the dance together, but maybe she was too late in being nice to him after all.

"Since I was eleven years old, it's been, like, the only thing I've looked forward to," she continued melodramatically, not letting Brooke change the subject. "And now I'm going to have to be in school when practically no one else in our grade is. I'll probably have to eat lunch with Miss Morris. Can you think of anything worse?"

"No," Brooke replied honestly.

Louise felt like she was going to throw up, and she wasn't sure if it was because the lunchroom smelled even more strongly than usual of its nauseating combination of ammonia cleaning products, garlic, and burned Tater Tots or if she was *that* upset. Louise and Brooke weaved their way past the long rectangular tables with their attached red circular stools as they took their usual round corner seat by the window, deftly avoiding a spilled pool of low-fat Italian salad dressing—an embarrassing moment just waiting to happen.

"And I'm sure Tiff will be going," Brooke continued, sweeping a pile of crumbs off their table with a crumple of paper napkins. The janitors didn't clean up until after the last lunch shift, so the tables were always gross and sticky by this point in the afternoon.

"Can you please not make me feel so bad about this?" Louise pleaded as she dunked an orange fry from Brooke's tray in the pool of ketchup. Fine, the greasy fries did make her feel a little better.

"Sorry, maybe she'll get the flu," Brooke responded, snapping back into supportive-best-friend mode. "Or food poisoning," she continued, pointing accusingly at her brown plastic lunch tray filled with the typically inedible Fairview food. "Which is totally a possibility here."

"True," Louise agreed with a sigh.

"Anyway, think of it this way. You'll have a whole week to wear whatever crazy vintage ensemble you want without any fear of me making a single sarcastic remark. It could totally be worse."

"How?" Louise challenged, pointing a deep-fried potato spear at her friend accusingly.

"Someone could have died?" Brooke finally suggested, cracking a smile.

"Thanks," Louise said flatly.

"Hey, is anyone sitting here?" Todd dropped his scuffed skateboard and plunked down in the empty hard plastic chair next to Louise. His lunch tray was completely filled with two hamburgers, curly fries, a fudge brownie, and chocolate milk—a typical boy's lunch. Her stomach did a little somersault when the sleeve of Todd's sweatshirt brushed against her bare wrist.

"Aren't you going to eat with Tiff?" Louise asked, quickly moving her arm away. Brooke stomped down hard on Louise's canvas sneaker. "Ouch," she mumbled.

Todd looked at her, confused. "Why?" he asked, seemingly totally clueless.

"Never mind," she replied quietly. Maybe she *was* being a little bit paranoid.

"So, Paris…how awesome is that going to be?" Todd asked. If he could have said exactly the wrong thing, that would be it.

"I'm not going," Louise blurted out, biting hard on her lower lip.

"Bummer," he said, scarfing down a fistful of fries. Louise's mind immediately began overanalyzing that one mumbled word. Was he actually upset or was he just saying that? She watched him devour his hot lunch in the un-self-conscious way that only boys could. Louise could never get herself to eat a school hamburger. The texture was just too gross to think about. During the school day, she considered herself a vegetarian.

"Matt!" Todd yelled, jumping up from his seat. "Yo, did you see that kick-flip I did earlier today by the bleachers?" He shoved the rest of the burger in his mouth. "See you guys later," he said through a mouthful of chewed food as he grabbed his skateboard, and left Louise and Brooke sitting at the table with his half-eaten tray of food. As though they were supposed to clean up for him?

"Yeah, bummer," she replied. Louise was so confused. Maybe it was too unrealistic to think that she and Todd could be anything aside from what they already were. Which was *what*, exactly?

CHAPTER 8

If Louise wasn't prone to acts of melodrama, she would be forced to admit there actually was one other thing she had been looking forward to besides the seventh-grade class trip—the Traveling Fashionista Vintage Sale. It was coming up this weekend, and it couldn't have arrived at a more perfect moment. Maybe instead of traveling to a different country, she could travel back to a different era again. Like, permanently—not counting being on the *Titanic*, Alice Baxter's life wasn't so bad. It was actually pretty fabulous, come to think of it. Louise prayed there was more than one magical dress in the shop. And that she hadn't made up this whole thing in her head. If the time traveling did really happen, she was a little nervous that she might end up stuck in another risky predicament, but the fear was pushed aside by the fact that right now she needed a long vacation from her life.

The invitation said this sale wasn't at the Chapel Street

location like it had been last time, hence, she guessed, the *traveling* part. Well, at least one interpretation of it. The new location definitely added to the enigma of the experience. You couldn't just pop in and pick up a vintage quilted Chanel purse whenever you wanted; they had to choose you. Number 37 Spring Street was another unfamiliar address in her small town, which was weird, as Louise thought she knew every square inch of the place by now. She typed the coordinates into her iPhone and waited for the highlighted route to appear. But nothing did except an error message. According to her GPS, 37 Spring Street in Fairview, Connecticut, didn't even exist?!

"Mom, do you know where Spring Street is?" Louise asked, bounding into the kitchen.

"What, dear?" Mrs. Lambert was staring off into space as she sat at the enormous blond oak kitchen table that was strewn with paperwork. A delicate blue-and-white china teacup was poised in midair as though she had forgotten halfway that she wanted a sip of Earl Grey.

"Spring Street," Louise repeated. These days, her mom was even more distracted than usual, which was saying something.

"That's funny, I noticed it just this morning on my errands," Mrs. Lambert replied, coming back down to planet Earth and placing the cup carefully on its saucer. "I think it's a new street—well, more of an alley, really, by the back entrance to the post office. Why do you ask?"

"There's another vintage sale there today. I thought I could get something for Brooke's thirteenth birthday party next weekend. She's doing a fancy-dress theme."

"How lovely," her mom replied absentmindedly.

Lovely? Was she even listening to her? For once in her life, her mother wasn't putting up a fight about vintage. Louise felt like she had spent the past year constantly defending her thrift-store purchases to her mother. Louise assumed it was her posh English upbringing that made it impossible for Mrs. Lambert to fathom why her daughter would actually choose to shop at a secondhand store. And considering that Louise had fainted at the last sale, she had assumed that this visit would be a much tougher sell.

So why wasn't she upset with her now for bringing in those old clothes contaminated with their ancient germs and possibly killing off the family with scarlet fever or bubonic plague or some other old-fashioned disease like her mother always said? Something really must be wrong. She wished her mother would snap out of it and act like her old self again. This robot mom was starting to give Louise the creeps.

"I guess I won't have to get any new outfits for the Paris

trip, right?" she asked wistfully, hoping that somehow she could persuade her distracted mother to change her mind.

Mrs. Lambert's gaze suddenly snapped back into focus. "You know where we stand on this issue. I'm sorry, I really am, but the answer is still no," she replied firmly, nervously playing with the single strand of classic pearls around her neck. Louise wondered if her mother, with her fancy childhood of au pairs and maid service, had ever been told no about *anything* at Louise's age. Definitely nothing this major. This trip was crucial for Louise's social development. She had to make them understand that.

"It's not fair!" she blurted out.

"Louise Ann Lambert!" Oh no, her full name, never a good sign. "I'm sorry, but the reality is we need to cut back on our expenses, and a trip to Europe is not in the cards right now. A lot of people have much worse problems. It wouldn't kill you to be a little more understanding. This isn't easy on any of us."

"But you don't get how important this is!" was the only thing Louise could think of to say.

"You need to put this in perspective and stop acting like a spoiled brat!"

Louise's mouth dropped. Way harsh.

"Oh, dear, I didn't mean that. I'm under a lot of stress right now. I'm sorry, dahling. Let's make popcorn on the stove and watch Audrey Hepburn in *Roman Holiday* tonight like we used to. I could use a holiday."

"I have homework," Louise said, sulking, even though it was Saturday and that was one of their all-time favorite black-and-white films.

"Please, Louise, be careful! And don't forget your cell," her mother instructed with an unexpected urgency.

Louise stormed out of the kitchen more determined than ever to track down Marla and Glenda and escape into the fantasy of their vintage collection—maybe this time for good.

CHAPTER 9

Louise sat on the banana seat of her three-speed pink bike and looked over at her home from the road. The large Tudor-style house, set back uphill on its neatly manicured lawn, gave off an imposing air. From the outside you would never know of the recent turmoil and worry taking place within its stone walls. The only hint that something was slightly amiss was her dad's car parked in the driveway during the workweek.

She waved at her neighbor Mrs. Weed pruning her rose-bushes, as she did every Saturday afternoon, and pedaled through the familiar tree-lined streets downtown toward the post office. As Louise rode through her hometown with the streamers from her bike's handlebars flapping in the breeze, she felt a sickening combination of nostalgia and restlessness. Every single memory she had was inextricably linked to these streets, houses, and people, and it felt both comforting and claustrophobic at the same time.

The sign for Spring Street was distinctive, not only because it was hand-painted in black letters on a wooden post that she had never seen before, but also because it marked the beginning of a cobblestone path. Pretty much every other road in her town was paved and modern. This already felt like she was going back in time. Louise pushed up the sleeves of her cardigan and pedaled determinedly down the bumpy and uneven lane.

Tall, thick oak trees shaded the street from the bright afternoon sun, and the farther she rode, the darker and narrower the path became. Louise prided herself on being an explorer and was amazed that such a peculiar street, only a fifteen-minute bike ride from her house, had eluded her. Maybe her town wasn't quite as small as she had thought.

She stopped in front of the first white mailbox she came to, illogically numbered 37 in chipped green paint, and double-checked her invitation. This had to be the place.

Turning down the driveway, she approached a small stone cottage. To Louise, this seemed like a very odd place to have a pop-up store. But, she reminded herself, she was dealing with two rather unusual shopkeepers.

Suddenly, just as she reached the end of the drive, her bike's back tire got caught in the uneven gravel, depositing Louise abruptly on her side with her heavy bike crumpled on top of her on the overgrown front lawn. *Ouch.* Another glamorous entrance.

She disentangled herself from the pink metal frame, brushed the dirt off her scraped knee, and looked around to see if anyone else had caught that embarrassing moment. She was most definitely alone. Louise cautiously walked up the softly rotting wooden steps to the arched mahogany door, trying to ignore the pounding feeling in her left temple. As she lifted the heavy brass door knocker, she felt a moment of intense trepidation, a sudden heart-racing fear of the unknown. She triple-checked the teal invitation to make sure she was in the right spot. Louise had wanted to go to the sale by herself to assert her independence in some way, but she was now wishing that she had her best friend by her side, like she did the first time. *Why exactly am I doing this again? Didn't this experience almost, like, kill me the last time?* But before she could turn around and get back on her bike, she heard the tinkling of bells, and the heavy door swung open before her. Louise instinctively stepped into the darkness.

CHAPTER 10

"Marla! How absolutely fabulous! Our favorite Traveling Fashionista has returned!"

"I told you she'd be back, now, didn't I, Glenda?"

Before Louise could even utter a hello, the ladies rushed toward her, pulling her into the dimly lit cottage, two sets of iridescent green eyes gleaming with excitement. The wide-plank wooden floor was strewn with loose sequins and lost buttons, and Louise's high-top neon pink Converse crunched down on them when she stepped across the threshold.

"Hope it wasn't too out of the way. Glad you could find us," Glenda trilled, petting the top of Louise's frizzy head like she was an obedient cat. She pulled a long blade of grass out of Louise's tousled bun. "Forget something?" she asked with a chuckle.

What Louise *had* almost forgotten was how tall and intimidating Glenda was, further accentuated by the stacked heels on her worn black leather Edwardian boots. Her wild red hair was not to be restrained by the tortoiseshell haircombs sticking up from the back of her head like antennae, which almost brushed the low wooden-beam ceilings.

"Where did this place come from?" Louise asked in awe. "My phone couldn't find it on a map."

"How on earth would your phone use a map?" Marla asked, puzzled, pushing her reading glasses up onto the bridge of her nose, magnifying her squinty green eyes. "Why, it was right here all along. I suppose sometimes you simply need someone to put up a sign," she said, slipping Louise's Anthropologie—but still vintage-looking—indigo cashmere cardigan off her shoulders and placing it on a padded hanger in a random rolling rack of clothing.

Marla and Louise were now the same height. Had Marla shrunk or had Louise grown? She couldn't be sure, but Louise now found herself staring directly at the wart that was at nose level with her own. (Nose, not wart.)

"Will I...will I get it back?" Louise asked. That was her favorite blue sweater; it went with everything and had these cool little buttons that looked like miniature pearls.

"Of course, dahling. We know exactly where everything is," Glenda replied, putting on a full-length leopard-print coat she'd plucked off the same rack. "Just where I left it!"

Louise found that hard to believe.

The one-room stone cottage was much larger than it had appeared from the outside and had been miraculously transformed into a shop bursting with clothes. Every square inch of space was jam-packed with vintage treasures. There were even button-up boots and high-heeled T-strap shoes piled high in the hearth. A colorfully ornate Venetian glass chandelier hung dangerously low from the center beam and cast off a sparkly light in the otherwise dim and shadowy store. The room smelled like mothballs and cedar, much like her mother's linen closet at home.

Louise thought it would save Marla and Glenda a lot of hassle to find one permanent location, but she couldn't help but love the air of mystery that surrounded the whole production. She recognized an ivory-colored armoire in the far corner from the last Fashionista Sale. That was definitely the closet where she had found her pink dress. She thought this was as good a time as any to ask them about what truly happened to her when she tried on that gown at the sale at 220 Chapel Street.

"Do you know an actress by the name of Miss Baxter?" Louise started, not quite sure how to phrase the question without sounding like a total nut.

"Alice Baxter?" Glenda asked with a raised eyebrow. "Perhaps. But we never discuss our clients, sweet pea."

"Yes, we sign a confidentiality agreement with everyone

who comes into our shop. I have it in here somewhere," Marla declared, rushing over to her rolltop desk and rummaging through a precarious stack of disorganized papers. "In fact, if I ever find it, I think it's time we have you sign one as well."

"Were you ever on the *Titanic*?" Louise asked bluntly.

Marla and Glenda exchanged a bemused look and then burst into laughter. "And just how old do you think we are?" Glenda asked, pausing. "On second thought, don't answer that. You do know that the *Titanic* sailed in the year 1912," she continued, giving Louise a searing look that strongly discouraged her from asking another follow-up question.

"You simply must have a look around. We have so much fabulous inventory for you to try on," Marla quipped, giving up on the lost paper and deftly changing the subject.

"Perhaps some music to enhance your shopping experience?" Glenda asked, putting a record on the old-fashioned phonograph that stood in the corner. The scratchy sounds of a jazz piano filled the air.

"Oooh, my favorite!" Marla and Glenda clasped hands and began twirling each other around the room, weaving in and out of the stacks of red-and-white-striped hatboxes and overstuffed coatracks, laughing and stirring up dust and glitter along the way. They certainly didn't need Louise to entertain them.

Walking farther into the room, Louise almost tripped over

a low Victorian-style chaise lounge that was covered with a rainbow of designer dresses from different decades. She immediately recognized a pink-and-green-patterned Lilly Pulitzer shift dress.

She picked up a skintight black Azzedine Alaia minidress with a long zipper that seemed to serve no other function than to look extremely awesome. Azzedine Alaia was one of the most famous couturiers of the eighties—he dressed all the hottest celebrities and supermodels.

These were the original supermodels, like Naomi Campbell, Cindy Crawford, and Stephanie Seymour. What if she tried this on and was transported or teleported or whatever it was back to the eighties in New York City? Maybe she was an art dealer or a singer like Madonna (whom Alaia also famously dressed). Who knows? Maybe she *was* Madonna, Louise thought, creating a whole story in her head. She could hang out downtown at the Mudd Club with iconic artists like Jean-Michel Basquiat and Andy Warhol. Besides, it was the eighties, the decade of excess. Shopping! Sushi! Monster cell phones! Excess sounded like exactly what Louise needed right about now.

While Marla and Glenda jitterbugged their way over to the other side of the store, Louise hid behind a pile of hatboxes, yanked off her Betsey Johnson white-and-pink floral sundress that she had scored for eight dollars on eBay, and wiggled her way into the micro-minuscule piece of stretchy black fabric. She would just take it for a little test-drive. Louise squinted her eyes shut and held out her arms in a T, waiting for that spinning dizzy feeling to take over her.

But apparently Louise wasn't destined to go anywhere. Maybe she *had* made up this whole thing in her mind after all. She opened her eyes to discover that she was right where she started at the Fashionista Sale with two glowering sales ladies staring down at her.

"You do know that shoplifting is a criminal offense in this state?" Marla questioned menacingly, toying with the poodle charm dangling from her neck by a thick gold chain. It was the same peculiar necklace she and Glenda each had worn the last time Louise was at the sale.

"Isn't it, Glenda? Or is that another state?" she asked, turning to her wide-eyed companion with a shrug.

"I was going to pay for it," Louise insisted abashedly.

"Now, dahling, who said anything about money? You didn't think we could let you leave the house in that hot little number, did you?" Glenda asked, peering behind the hatboxes with a disapproving glare. The jazz record had magically stopped with a screech and Louise was painfully aware of the silent judgment being passed on her.

Louise blushed as she looked down. She had to admit she looked a lot like Julia Roberts in the old romantic comedy *Pretty Woman*, premakeover.

"That little man is a genius, but Azzedine never did know when to stop snipping, did he?"

"Perhaps when you're a little older, my dear," Marla said more gently, brushing some mousy brown wisps from her eyes and handing Louise an elaborately embroidered silk kimono to wrap around herself. Louise hesitantly slipped on the teal-colored robe. Was she going to wake up and find herself as a geisha in Japan? What exactly was magical in the store, anyway? Maybe she'd dreamed the whole *Titanic* experience after all. She started to feel a little silly that she'd secretly been hoping she'd be able to try on a dress and escape into another person's life.

"How about this marvelous gown?" Glenda asked, holding out a hideous maroon puffy-sleeved crushed velvet dress that looked like it could be worn only at a renaissance fair.

"I think I'll pass," Louise replied, slightly distressed that her stylists were becoming as strict as her own mother. Didn't she get to choose her own adventure? Would she even get another adventure?

"Why, haven't we gotten picky, princess...?" Glenda tsked, tossing the dress onto the floor.

"Sorry, I guess I'm in a bad mood. My dad lost his job, my

mother and I just had a major fight, and I can't go on the school trip to Paris with the rest of my French class. They're so unfair. I never get to go anywhere."

"Well, that's not quite true, is it, dear?" Marla asked. Louise recognized then that "they're so unfair" had become her new mantra.

"In fact, I would say you've already traveled quite a bit more and farther than most young ladies these days." Glenda tittered. Wait, so they *did* know about her trip on the *Titanic*! "Let's forget about all that and find you something special to wear. As my dear friend Coco Chanel once said, 'There are people who have money and people who are rich.' If you could just appreciate all you have for a moment, you would realize that you, darling, are rich."

"I think right now I'd rather have money," Louise said, forlorn. Being rich, whatever that meant, wasn't exactly getting her a round-trip ticket to Paris, which at this point in her life seemed to have turned into one of her objectives, if not her sole one. "And didn't Coco Chanel die almost fifty years ago?" Louise asked, puzzled as to how Glenda and the iconic fashion designer Coco could be such close friends.

"Green goddess dip?" Marla interrupted, gracefully swooping around the cluttered room with a platter of crudités and a scary-looking bowl filled with a moldy green substance. "It's a family recipe. I whipped some up particularly for you!" she exclaimed, holding the tray up under Louise's nose.

Last year? Louise was tempted to ask. The limp carrot and celery sticks were fanned out in an arc around the terrifying-looking accoutrement. Louise immediately flashed back to the last time she'd sampled some of Marla's cooking experiments, and politely refused. Although what if, like her mother believed, it actually was the food poisoning that had brought on such vivid dreams of the *Titanic*? Before she had a chance to change her mind, Marla responded huffily, "Suit yourself!" and dropped the untouched appetizer in an open red-and-white-striped hatbox and swiftly shut the lid.

CHAPTER 11

"Now, I bet you've never seen anything like this in your vintage books," Glenda predicted, pushing a rolling rack of pastel taffeta-skirted ball gowns out of the way to reveal a locked glass case in the far corner of the room. The tall, clear box contained a lone robin's egg blue ball gown that looked as though it were suspended in air. A hazy beam of afternoon light filtering in through the small cottage window illuminated the dress perfectly, giving it an almost mystical quality. Louise gasped.

"The Met would love to get their hands on this *fabuloussss* number," Glenda rasped under her breath.

The dress was made of a delicate pale blue satin, the color of a Tiffany's box. The ruched bodice let out into a beautiful, full, long hoop skirt, decorated with two swooping panels that looked like stage curtains held together with gold tassels. Its plunging sweetheart neck was lined with an intricate white lace and royal blue ribbon trim, which also lined the bottom of the floor-length gown. The handmade lace also ran down the three-quarter-length sleeves in perfect ruffled rows and was finished with a large diamond-broached blue silk ribbon decorating each arm. A line of pale pink decorative silk bows ran down the front of the gown in a neat little row. The structured dress was standing upright and appeared as if it were floating in the space.

"It's almost as old as you!" Marla squeaked to Glenda as she unlocked the case.

Glenda raised a penciled-in eyebrow. "Ha. Ha," she said flatly, not laughing in the slightest.

"Who designed this?" Louise asked, still holding her breath. She had never seen a dress like it, and the vintage fashion nerd in her was dying to know.

"This..." Glenda began, leaving room for a dramatic pause, "...is a genuine Rose...Bertin."

"A Rose who?" Louise asked, surprised at not recognizing the designer. With all her obsessive research, she thought she had at least heard of all the great couturiers at this point.

"Kids these days," Glenda responded, scrunching up her nose like she smelled something rotten.

"Brooke's fancy-dress party—isn't this perfect!" Marla exclaimed, not answering Louise's question.

"How do you know about that?" Louise asked, still unnerved

by Glenda's and Marla's uncanny ability to pick out exactly what she was searching for. Had she mentioned the theme of Brooke's thirteenth birthday party? Had she even mentioned that Brooke was having a birthday party? She didn't think so.

"It does seem perfect," she replied hesitantly, moving closer to the dress to get a better look. "But how did you get this? It looks like it should be on display at a museum, not a vintage shop."

"Now how would you be able to wear it in a museum?" Glenda asked with a puzzled expression. "They have so many rules in places like that."

"But what if I rip it? It looks so fragile."

"Questions, questions! Why not a simple thank-you?" Marla interrupted, clicking her tongue in disapproval.

"Although it is not quite time for this one. Don't you agree, Marla?" Glenda asked in a low tone, giving her cohort a searing look. "As they say, timing is everything!"

"Very true, I do seem to lose track of time these days," Marla answered quickly, grabbing the rack of pastel-colored ball gowns again. "Perhaps you can try it on at the next sale, my dear?"

Louise gently ran her hand over the wispy blue fabric; it felt like it could crumble to dust between her fingers. How old was this piece? Technically speaking, she knew that a dress like this would be too old to be considered vintage. It was most definitely an antique and, in that case, extremely valuable.

Tiff Freedman would never wear something this awesome. Todd would be forced to fall back in love, or like, with Louise after seeing her in this dazzling pale blue gown. For one glorious night she could pretend like she was rich and could actually afford to have a couture dress like this made just for her.

"Please," Louise begged. "I'd really love to try this on."

The two women exchanged nervous glances, but before they had a chance to respond, there was a loud knocking at the front door. In a cloud of dust and clanging bells, an angry-looking Brooke burst into the cottage.

CHAPTER 12

"Brooke? What are you doing here?" Louise asked, stepping away from the glass vitrine in total shock. She was left with that weird feeling when two totally separate compartments of your life collide.

"Lou, I can't believe you didn't tell me you were coming to another Fashionista Sale! It's like you have a secret life or something. I thought we were best friends," she cried, throwing her hands up in total confusion.

"We are..."

"Your mother had to tell me where you were," Brooke added sadly, as though that were the ultimate betrayal. "I thought we shared everything. I know I don't really get your obsession with used clothes..."

Louise saw Glenda instinctively scowl. "We prefer the term *vintage*, sweetie. *Used* sounds so...déclassé."

"Okay." Brooke rolled her eyes, still standing in the doorway. "With vintage clothes. But I still wish you'd talk to me!"

"Oh, dear," Marla mumbled, quickly shoving the clothing rack of strapless gowns back in front of the glass case.

"I j-just…" Louise stuttered, not sure how she was going to talk her way out of this one.

"Brooke, my dear. How fabulously unexpected to see you again!" Glenda exclaimed in a much more chipper tone, quickly walking over and putting a protective arm around the distressed girl's shoulders.

"You see, Louise didn't want to tell you she was coming to visit us, as she wanted to surprise you with her dress for your party," Marla added, stroking Brooke's blonde head reassuringly.

"Wait, what are you wearing? Is *that* the outfit you plan on wearing to my birthday party?" Brooke asked, wide-eyed.

Louise looked down at her half-Japanese, half-eighties ensemble, now totally embarrassed. She'd forgotten about the bizarre kimono/minidress combination she was rocking.

"Not exactly," she answered, blushing.

"Now what in heavens are *you* wearing?" Glenda asked loudly, stepping back to examine Brooke's pink Juicy Couture hooded sweatshirt and black leggings, which were totally normal and cool at Fairview. Glenda shuddered as she ran her long crooked fingers along the velour fabric as though the sweatshirt were an alien artifact from the planet Bubble Gum. She took a peek at the tag in the collar.

"Juicy *Couture*? Ha! Let me show you what *couture* really means!" Glenda exclaimed, dramatically shaking her crazy red hair.

"I think we have something from a little designer named Karl Lagerfeld that would look smashing on you."

"Sure." Brooke shrugged indifferently, sending Louise a pointed look.

While Marla and Glenda guided Brooke over to the other side of the store to show her their extensive selection of Karl Lagerfeld for Chanel, Louise quietly tiptoed behind the rack of chiffon to the vitrine and slowly opened the thin glass-paned door. She held her breath, half expecting an alarm to sound or a net to drop down from the ceiling over her head, but nothing happened. Something inside her told her that she needed to try on the magnificent antique dress and that this might be her only opportunity.

She slid off the teal silk kimono and struggled to peel off the ridiculously skintight Alaia before the others caught on. She felt drawn to this glass box, as strongly as if the material itself were whispering her name. The exquisitely embroidered satin fabric was clearly hand sewn, and the artistry that went into the ethereal design took Louise's breath away.

She plucked the enormous robin's egg blue gown from its

installation, and a chill ran down her arms. Louise recognized that same prickly feeling from the last time, when she found the iridescent pink dress that had transported her back to the *Titanic*. An overwhelming wave of déjà vu washed over her.

"Darling, Louise! Brooke found something fabulous for you!" a raspy voice exclaimed from the other side of the crowded room. "Have you seen these adorable red Ferragamo wedges we left for you in the fireplace? Classics! And just your size! Where are you, dear?"

"I'll be right there!" Louise shouted, trying to sound as normal as possible. She quietly stepped into the structured hoop skirt and shimmied the blue satin top of the dress up snugly around her, slipping her left arm into a puckered silk sleeve. So far, the dress fit almost perfectly.

"Lou, you have to check these out!" she heard Brooke say as the sound of someone's footsteps started walking toward her.

"Come out, come out, wherever you are," Marla sang as the approaching footsteps continued to get louder and nearer. Louise was going to be discovered, and she was definitely going to be in trouble.

Without a moment to lose, she shoved her right hand inside the other teeny delicate armhole and was immediately blinded by a bright flash of sparkly blue-and-white light. With that, Louise instantly collapsed on the floor like a fancily dressed marionette whose strings had been cut.

"I don't design clothes.
I design dreams."

RALPH LAUREN,
American fashion designer

CHAPTER 13

When Louise awoke, she swore she was locked in a coffin. The air was still and stale, and she was crouched into a small wooden area that was as quiet as death. Her head ached and her body was sore, as if she had been frozen in this uncomfortably stiff position for hours. What had she gotten herself into this time?

Before she had a chance to ponder the question, a flood of sunlight abruptly filled the dark, stuffy space. *Ouch.* Louise rubbed her sleep-crusted eyes.

"My dear Gabrielle, what a marvelous hiding spot!"

Gab-who? A tiny white puffball jumped on Louise's skirts and began licking her hand and barking.

"If I didn't have my precious Macaroon, I don't think we would have ever found you. Good little puppy," a pretty blonde girl cooed, picking up the wisp of a dog and giving it a flurry of butterfly kisses on its nose. From Louise's limited closet-eye view, the girl was tiny with flushed pink cheeks, alabaster white skin, a slightly pronounced lower lip, and wide pale blue-gray eyes.

Louise looked around, trying to get her bearings. She was squatting on top of a pile of silk dresses in what appeared to be an armoire. Something sharp was digging into her backside. She reached down and discovered she was sitting on a diamond-encrusted buckle clasped to an old-fashioned lemon yellow high-heeled shoe.

By the looks of that curved heel, she suddenly realized that she might not be in the right century. Louise had a flashback to the sketch in her history notebook and could have sworn she had drawn a similar shoe in Miss Morris's class the other day. It was now a real object in her hand! She wished she had remembered to research it in her vintage book that night.

"Where am I?" Louise stuttered. Her voice sounded strange. *French?*

"Voilà!" the girl squealed, helping Louise to her shaky feet and leading her out into a marvelously decorated room. The light greenish-blue walls were inlaid with gold leaf detailing. A bronze-and-glass chandelier illuminated by dripping lit candles sparkled from the ceiling. Vases of pink-and-purple wildflowers were displayed on every available surface, and the flowers seemed to match the floral pattern in the needlepoint rug and gauzy muslin curtains that were fluttering in the ceiling-high open windows.

Louise blinked, trying to readjust to her new reality. The dress had actually worked! She wondered if anyone knew where she was.

"Your hair!" Louise exclaimed, surprised to see that the girl's light blonde hair was teased into a giant beehive that towered a good twelve inches above her head. Stuck into the nest of hair were two white ostrich feathers that extended the hairstyle another few feet. It was a bizarre and incredibly dramatic look, but if you subtracted the projectile hair, the girl was short, about the same height as Louise. She also noted happily that beneath the layers of her white muslin empire-waist dress the girl appeared to be skinny and flat-chested, just like she was.

"Do you think it's too much?" the girl asked, letting out a high-pitched giggle. "I think Leonard did a marvelous job with this pouf!"

"No, it's amazing," Louise quickly responded. "I've just never seen anybody have a hairstyle quite like that before."

"Well, then you should look in a mirror!" She laughed. "It seems we left you in the wardrobe for too long. Come, have some orange blossom tea and croissants in the garden. The girls are waiting for us."

Louise flashed back to her journey on the *Titanic* as Miss Alice Baxter and thought that as long as this girl was in the room, it was probably best that she *didn't* have a look in the

mirror. From her last experience, she learned that the mirror's reflection was the one place where her true identity was revealed for everyone to see.

"Ummm. Okay. The garden sounds lovely," Louise agreed, more confused than ever.

"Oh, dear, Gabrielle, your dress is a disaster. Why don't you change into one of these for now?" The girl held out a pale lavender tea dress made in flowing gauzy chiffon and crinkled muslin that she'd plucked from the floor of the armoire.

Clearly this girl was mistaking her for someone named Gabrielle. Whoever that was. Louise looked down at her blue dress, which was a crumpled mess and halfway hanging off of her, and realized it was a breathtaking brand-new version of the one she had secretly tried on at the Fashionista Sale. The dress was definitely the same, but the bustle was severely lopsided now and the fabric, which was a much more vibrant shade than it had been in the vintage store, was all wrinkled from crouching in the closet.

"This will be perfect. That other style was so stiff anyway. I'm getting rather bored with all of this formality. I plan on banning corsets from Petit Trianon for good," the gregarious girl said, rolling her eyes like any other twenty-first-century teenager.

Wait, Petit what? Where exactly was she? Wherever she was, it already seemed a lot more amazing than a class trip to

France, Louise thought, looking around at the room, which was decorated with rose-colored, silk-upholstered love seats and foot stools and marble-topped tables. There was a large gold harp positioned in the center of the room next to a stand covered in sheet music, as though someone had just finished a lesson.

"Go change now. I'll wait," the girl ordered, yanking off the rest of Louise's blue dress. She directed an embarrassed Louise, now wearing only a stiff old-fashioned undergarment, toward an ornately decorated changing screen that was hand painted with finely stenciled hummingbirds and flowers.

She didn't want to leave the magical dress, but she didn't seem to have a choice in the matter. Something about this girl's bossy tone suggested that she wasn't used to taking no for an answer. Louise made a quick mental plan to hide the gown in the wardrobe underneath the other dresses so she would always know where it was. Then she could go back to her life in Connecticut whenever she wanted since she now knew the magic was embedded in the fabric of the vintage dress. Hopefully that was how it still worked, she thought to herself with trepidation. She was definitely a long way from home.

"The palace is so beautiful," Louise commented from the other side of the partition as she struggled to unlace the corseted cream-colored bodice, hoping to get a clue as to where she was.

"Palace? This is my playhouse, silly." The girl giggled again. "Are you almost ready? Let's get you some air. Those corsets are affecting the blood flow to your brain. I do wish that we could always wear our tea dresses."

On second thought, if this was considered a playhouse, Louise never wanted to go home. It was the fanciest room she had ever been in—even the doorknobs looked like they were made of gold! *This girl must have piles of money.*

When Louise was little, she had drawn detailed plans of her dream playhouse. It had a rose garden, secret passageways, a water slide, and a tea room. When she showed these blueprints to her dad, he said he'd get someone working on it right away. Louise didn't realize he was just playing along when she really meant it. Apparently, when this girl asked for a playhouse, someone listened. They took her seriously even though she was just a teenager and built her the most fabulous playhouse ever, one that was even more magnificent than most people's homes, while Louise ended up building a fort with bedsheets and cardboard boxes in her walk-in closet and serving imaginary tea to her Barbie dolls.

"Your Highness?" A woman in a scarlet-and-silver uniform and crisp white apron walked in, averting her eyes and curtseying.

"*Oui?*" the girl responded nonchalantly.

This girl answered to *Your Highness*? She must be a princess, which meant Louise was now apparently friends with royalty. *Awesome!*

"Tea is served."

CHAPTER 14

"*Pardonnez-moi.* This just arrived from your mother in Austria."

Another scarlet-uniformed servant had walked into the room and, with a slight curtsey, offered the beehive-haired girl a thick white envelope from a sterling silver tray. She grabbed the envelope and carelessly ripped it open, then sat down on a powder pink upholstered love seat, concentrating intently on the words, her finger slowly tracing underneath the individual letters as though reading was a great challenge for her. As the princess gradually made her way down the page, Louise saw tears welling up in the corners of her blue-gray eyes. She abruptly threw down the letter in a fit and ran out of the room.

What just happened? Louise wondered, picking up the tear-stained parchment lying on the needlepoint carpet. She quickly read the letter, which was written in thick black calligraphy ink.

My dearest daughter,

Do not be negligent about your appearance. . . . I cannot caution you enough against letting yourself slip into the errors that the members of the French royal family have fallen into of late. They may be good and virtuous, but they have forgotten how to appear in public, how to set the tone 'for the nation.' . . . I therefore beg you, both as your tender mother and as your friend, not to give in to any further shows of nonchalance about your appearance or court protocol. If you do not heed my advice, you will regret it, but it will be too late. On this point alone you must not follow your 'French' family's example. It is up to you now to set the tone at Versailles.

Whoa, this was not exactly the most nurturing or understanding message coming from her "tender mother." This young girl was expected to set the tone...at Versailles...through her clothing choices? Louise felt a slight jolt of recognition. Louise's mother may have given her a hard time about her vintage clothing, but this sounded almost like a threat! Why was the girl's mom writing her letters, anyway? Didn't she live with her? Wait, wasn't Miss Morris just lecturing about Versailles? Louise's mind was racing. This girl seemed so young to be living away from home, although maybe she was better off, as this lady sounded more like a wicked stepmother.

She discreetly set the letter down on the pink velvet love seat and left the room to try to find the princess. Maybe Louise could comfort her. Stepping into a grand black-and-white-tiled entry hall, Louise's breath got caught in her throat. She was immediately confronted with a gilded arched mirror hung above the teak hall table on the opposite wall. She didn't want to look, but she couldn't help it. It was as though there were a magnetic field drawing her in. Slowly, Louise walked over to see her reflection.

She was expecting this, but still it was jarring. She was immediately confronted with the image of her twelve-year-old self hesitantly smiling at her from the other side of the glass, frizzy hair and all, dressed up in a lavish purple gown. To see her familiar brace-face staring back at her from the cloudy mirror was both comforting and depressing. She hadn't had time to miss her old self yet and turned around quickly to make sure no one else was watching her.

Louise hurried out of the grand French doors, running

away from her reflection in the mirror, and discovered she was in a beautiful garden that looked like it was out of a children's fairy tale. A round table was set with delicate pink china plates and teacups and a blue-and-white porcelain pitcher filled with freshly cut white lilies and fragrant purple lilacs. Platters of tea cakes and pots of bright red jam were scattered around on the white linen tablecloth. Little yellow honeybees darted around the sweet red raspberry jelly.

Two ladies were sitting at the table. One girl looked to be around Louise's age. She had pale skin, soft blue eyes, and golden blonde hair done up in a less dramatic version of the princess's. She was wearing a muslin dress like Louise's, but hers was pale green. The other woman was much older, with drab brown hair and hard steel-colored eyes, and was dressed in a more formal, stiff, long-sleeved beige dress. She had a heavy build, and her wrists looked like they were squeezed into their sleeves like sausages stuffed in a silk casing. Maybe she was the chaperone or something.

Louise instinctively patted her own head, which was getting kind of itchy, and was surprised to feel it was also arranged into a stiff pile of hair weaved into a wig of even more hair. It felt kind of like a horse's tail. She reached in and pulled out a sharp metal wire. Was that supposed to be there? Judging from the coarse, matted texture, Louise had a feeling she did not want to know the last time this Gabrielle girl had washed her hair.

"Macaroon found her—in the wardrobe!" the princess exclaimed, walking up to the table and wiping the last tear from her cheek as she dropped the shih tzu carelessly on the grass near two small white-and-brown lapdogs that were barking and frolicking around. "Wasn't that clever? I do love a good game. Let's play again after tea." A lone baby goat wandered up to the clearing, and the princess fed it a small cake from the table, which it greedily devoured, licking the remnants from her bare hand as she giggled.

"Marvelous!" The light blonde–haired girl nodded and clapped in agreement.

Louise smiled, trying to act like nothing out of the ordinary was happening. As though this was exactly where she was supposed to be. The girls looked as if they could be in high school, but they still loved to play hide-and-seek and have tea parties in the garden of their enormous playhouse with live farm animals roaming in and out of the idyllic tableau. Maybe if Louise stayed here forever she wouldn't have to grow up after all. She could still be a kid. Even when she turned thirteen.

They waited until the princess was seated before they started pouring the steaming hot tea and grabbing at the pastries.

"This is the most beautiful playhouse I've ever been to!" Louise exclaimed, buttering a flaky croissant.

"Isn't it lovely?" the princess sighed. "I wish we could stay here forever. I never want to go back to Versailles. Louis knew how much the etiquette and formality at the palace tried my patience, so he gave this to me as a gift. *At the Petit Trianon, I am me!*"

Louise looked out at the grounds. The table was in the clearing of a beautiful garden that grew wild and lush with roses and lilies. The garden was on the edge of a large, still lake that was flanked on one side by a wooden footbridge. Cows and sheep wandered around freely, chomping on the wild grasses. There were orange blossom trees and rosebushes planted randomly around them, but somehow it all seemed to work perfectly. Across the way, a woman dressed in a long gray muslin dress carrying a silver metal milk pail was walking a cow on a leash made of blue silk ribbon that was tied in a bow around its neck. It seemed like they were in the middle of the English countryside, but Louise knew from the letter that this was France. Everything was almost too perfect, more like they were in the middle of someone's idea of the countryside, like this couldn't really exist in real life.

Across the clearing, Louise caught the eye of a cute young gardener with rich, wavy chestnut brown hair and wearing dark breeches and a waistcoat who was pruning some rosebushes with a large pair of clippers. He quickly looked away, blushing, as though he didn't want to make eye contact with her. Maybe this Gabrielle was homely or cross-eyed or something? She tried not to take it too personally.

"Who's that?" she whispered, nodding toward him. Maybe he was already flirting with one of these girls.

The giggling stopped, and the table fell totally pin-drop silent. "Who?" the princess finally asked, as though there were no one standing just a few feet away.

"The guy over there," Louise clarified. "Trimming the rosebushes."

More silence. Louise felt her cheeks get hot as the girls stared at her curiously. Then the table erupted into laughter, as though she had just told the funniest joke they had ever heard. "Isn't she a riot?" the princess said.

"Gabrielle has such a marvelous sense of humor," the girl in the green remarked. Louise lowered her head. She didn't get it.

"Gabrielle, can you please pass the sugar to the Princesse de Lamballe?" the princess asked after the giggles had subsided. She handed Louise a delicate white porcelain sugar bowl with a miniature sterling silver spoon sticking out of it. Wait, didn't that name sound familiar, too?

Louise looked around the garden table at the other girl and the woman, neither of whom was giving her any clues as to whose tea needed sugar. Was the princess Brown Dress or Green Dress? Gabrielle should definitely know the answer to that question, but the real Louise had no clue.

After a few moments' hesitation, she handed the sugar to Brown Dress, whose stiff posture and haughty demeanor made her appear a bit more regal, who then passed it across the table to Green Dress with a slightly confused look. Whoops. Green Dress, the Princesse de Lamballe, put one heaping spoonful in her tea and looked over at Louise. "Now that's a roundabout way of doing things, isn't it?"

Brown Dress gave Louise a long, puzzled look. Louise felt like the woman could see right through her. She took a sip of sweet orange tea and tried to ignore the older woman's intense gaze by concentrating on spreading jam on her bread, like filling every nook and cranny with red goo was the most important task in the world. Blending in was going to be a little harder than she'd anticipated. She was going to have to be a lot more careful.

Suddenly there was a commotion of pounding hooves and barking dogs. A pack of beagles followed by five men on horseback wearing navy blue riding coats with big gold buttons and red-and-white trim rode up to the garden gate.

Macaroon and the other two dogs yipped wildly and darted under the table, hiding under the women's long dresses. The other ladies started giggling and blushing and basically transforming into blubbering bubbleheads, as though these were

popular eighth-grade lacrosse players coming over to sit at their lunch table. The men all looked old to Louise and not nearly as cute as her new crush, who was still nearby, now on his knees weeding the flower beds, which she knew because she was still kind of watching him out of the corner of her eye.

"My dear wife," the porkiest one of them called out in a wheezing, nasally voice. He took off his three-cornered hat with a big white feather sticking out of it to reveal a very stylized hairdo curled up on the sides and tied back in a thick ponytail and secured with a black silk ribbon.

Please, Louise silently prayed, *may this man not be talking to Gabrielle.*

She was more than a little surprised to hear the princess respond sweetly, "*Oui, mon chéri?*"

Whoa, this gorgeous teenage girl was already married. *And to that guy?*

"I would be honored if you could meet me at the palace tonight at half past seven. We are receiving some Swedish military dignitaries and it would be best if you could make it." He was asking her, but in a way that made it clear that she'd better be there, kind of the way Louise felt when the princess asked her to change her dress. Even though it was posed as a question, she really didn't have a choice in the matter.

"Of course, I would be delighted," the princess responded flatly. She was the only one at the table not flustered by the men's dramatic arrival. In fact, she seemed almost bored. "We look forward to it. Enjoy your hunt."

Brown Dress and the Princesse de Lamballe seemed to be too busy coquettishly hiding behind their fans and fluttering their eyelashes at the other men to notice the change in the princess's demeanor.

"Wonderful. See you then," he replied in his winded tone. He clumsily returned the old-fashioned hat to his head, nearly falling off his speckled brown horse in the process. A little giggle escaped the princess's sealed lips.

Louise bit her lip, wondering what French royal family she was dining with who could be so peculiar.

With that awkward spectacle, he and the rest of his hunting party rode off into the woods in a cloud of dust and the cacophony of yapping dogs.

CHAPTER 15

"I suppose that I must get prepared to welcome the foreign court. We shall postpone our games until tomorrow," the princess announced in a somber tone that sounded as though she were getting ready for a funeral, not a party. The sun was shining high in the cloudless sky and it appeared to be the middle of the afternoon. Wasn't the party tonight? How long did this girl take to get ready?

"Let me accompany you," the Princesse de Lamballe offered eagerly, rising to her feet. She seemed to want any excuse to be of service to her. As she waved her fan, Louise could make out her flushed pink cheeks and easy smile. The Princesse de Lamballe smoothed down her fluttering spring green chiffon dress, and the two girls linked arms like they were best friends.

"*Merci beaucoup*, my dear heart. We will see you, Gabrielle, and Madame Adelaide this evening at half past seven. Please don't be late." She bid *au revoir* to Louise and the other woman, who was apparently named Adelaide. Louise was expected at a fancy party for royalty and foreign dignitaries. How cool was that? In the course of a few hours and quite possibly a few hundred years, her social life had suddenly gotten way more exciting.

The girls left the garden with Macaroon and the other little dogs loyally trailing after them. Louise realized she was now seated alone at the table with this other woman, who on closer inspection looked old enough to be Louise's mother. She was looking at her in a way that made Louise feel like she had spinach stuck between her two front teeth.

"Perhaps I should be going as well," Louise finally announced, feeling uncomfortable under her companion's silent, penetrating gaze. She began collecting the crumb-dusted plates to clear the table, a habit ingrained from her other life, where mothers expected their children to do that sort of thing, but she stopped abruptly when she saw the woman's confused look. Louise carefully set down the tower of teacups, realizing that if she was at a palace, there were probably people who were supposed to do this for them.

As if on cue, the woman in the apron who had announced teatime earlier walked out of the playhouse carrying a large empty silver tray and a starched white dish towel draped over her arm along with three other women in matching scarlet-

and-silver uniforms trailing behind her. Whoever this Gabrielle was, she definitely did not do dishes. Therefore Louise had to remember that she no longer did dishes, and that probably applied to all other chores as well. *Nice.* She could get used to this.

"We shall go together; our apartments are adjoining. It only makes sense."

Arghh, great. She was never going to be able to lose this lady. On the other hand, Louise rationalized, it was good to have someone lead her to Gabrielle's room, as she had absolutely no idea how to get there. Judging by the enormous size of these grounds, she could be walking around lost all day, and this was a party she did not want to miss.

"The dauphine always looks so beautiful, does she not?" Madame Adelaide asked as she closed the tall iron-and-gold gate leading to the grand playhouse. They strolled together through the magnificent gardens.

Dauphine? What or who was that? Louise had to assume she was talking about the princess.

"Yes, she does," she enthusiastically agreed.

"It's a shame that it can't last forever," Adelaide remarked cryptically, sneaking a look over at Louise as if to gauge her reaction.

"Yes, it is," Louise agreed again, for lack of something better to say. What did that mean? She really did not want to make small talk with this woman for fear of saying the wrong thing, and besides, she was more than a little distracted by the fabulous landscape she was walking through.

Louise took in a deep breath of sweet lilac- and honeysuckle-scented fresh air. These gardens were like no others she had seen before. They were much more organized than the loose, wild-hamlet feeling of Petit Trianon. Rows of topiary trees were pruned into neat geometric shapes. They walked quietly down a wide, white-pebbled path lining a vast carpet of neatly trimmed grass, past dozens of gleaming marble urns and statues, perfectly carved figures that looked like they belonged in a museum, not on a garden road. Creamy marble benches were placed periodically next to the paths underneath poplar trees so that one could sit in the shade and admire the beds of blooming roses and jasmine alongside reflecting pools. She heard chirping songbirds and rushing water spurting from the numerous fountains. There was a slight rustling in the bushes, and Louise thought she caught a glimpse of that same cute gardener darting behind a topiary bush. She certainly wouldn't mind running into him again. Maybe he would have some insight into exactly who Louise, or rather, this Gabrielle woman, was.

They eventually arrived at two enormous rectangular pools of water, larger than any Olympic-size swimming pool Louise had ever swum in (although obviously these were more for decoration than swim practice). Four bronze statues of some mythological figures adorned the corners of each pool. The afternoon sun reflecting off each body of water was almost blinding. She shaded her eyes with her hand and slowly looked up to behold the most magnificent palace she had ever laid eyes on.

She heard her companion take in a sharp breath, apparently also overwhelmed by the beauty, even though unlike Louise she must have seen it at least a thousand times before.

"Versailles," Adelaide swooned. "Isn't it the most incredible vision?"

Versailles. Where have I heard that word before? Louise found herself wondering again. This was by far the most enormous and imposing structure she had ever encountered. The grand limestone castle seemed to go on in both directions for eternity. Massive arched, gold-paned windows with stately balconies that were flanked by ornate marble columns and classical statues ran along the upper and lower levels. Uniformed guards stood at rapt attention along the perimeter of the building.

Louise, mouth agape, looked as if she were trying to take in all the grandeur and beauty through her open lips. "Oh, yes," she finally answered. "This was truly worth the journey."

CHAPTER 16

Louise tried to keep up with Adelaide as they walked swiftly through the vast marble hallway to their wing of the palace while still attempting to check out all the fresco-painted ceilings, ornate wall detailing, and massive oil paintings. The enormous scale of the rooms and impressive art collection covering every available surface made her feel like she was walking through the Metropolitan Museum of Art in New York City. Madame Adelaide then abruptly excused herself, saying she must have forgotten her favorite silk gloves back at Petit Trianon. They must have been very special gloves, as that long walk to their apartments seemed to have taken them almost an hour.

Louise wanted to explore the palace before the party that evening. She was suddenly living in a castle in France—how could she *not* have a look around? She turned in the opposite direction than the older woman's and walked down a wide, deserted black-and-white-tiled arched hallway, her old-fashioned heeled purple mules making a satisfying click-ing noise on the marble floor. Grand twenty-foot-tall arched windows lined one side of the hall, exposing a limestone ter-race that overlooked a spectacular view of the gorgeous mani-cured gardens.

She almost tripped over a pack of yelping little lapdogs that ran wildly past her, sliding across the slippery marble in manic pursuit of a fluffy white Persian cat that had taken off running through the gold-leaf-plated corridor. Louise pinched her nose. She was starting to feel a little woozy. There was a strong overpowering scent unique to this place—a combination of talcum powder, orange blossom, and dog poo. It seemed to be both the fanciest and dirtiest place she had ever visited.

She peeked into the first room she came to on the right, as the door had been carelessly left slightly ajar. The doorway was so tall that Louise barely reached the gold-plated handle. She was starting to feel like a character in *Alice's Adventures in Wonderland*. The room was plastered with a busy floral wall-paper crawling with vines and bouquets of lilies and peacock feathers that matched the embroidered pattern on the bed coverlet and fixed wall hanging behind the fabric-covered headboard. A bust of the princess was prominently displayed on the mantel of the ornate fireplace underneath an oil paint-ing of a man with a George Washington–style hairdo who was wearing a navy-and-red uniform with gold buttons and whom Louise didn't recognize. Two crystal chandeliers hung down low on heavy golden chains from the oil-painted ceiling. A neoclassical-style mahogany jewelry cabinet stood against one wall right next to the faint outline of a little door that was almost completely camouflaged by the wallpaper. Louise would have to remember that secret exit if they ever played hide-and-seek in the palace.

She was surprised to see the dauphine, which she deduced meant "princess," standing barefoot on the shiny hardwood floor in the center of the grand room and wearing nothing more than a thin peach silk slip. Her arms were crossed protectively across her small frame, and she was surrounded by at least ten other women, including the Princesse de Lamballe, whom Louise initially recognized by her spearmint green gown now that her cherubic round face was no longer hidden behind her fan. Unlike the dauphine, all the other women were fully dressed in long dresses with wide hooped skirts and fitted bodices. The dauphine wasn't wearing much more than a chemise. Her ashy blonde hair was pulled back in a loose braid, and she had two circles of vibrant red rouge painted on her cheeks. Louise tried not to sneeze as an overwhelming whiff of powder and floral perfume tickled her nose. One of the women helped the dauphine into an intricate corset, and another lady tightly laced it up the back. It was as though each assistant had her own particular role to play. It was all very choreographed and organized, as if they performed this ritual every day. The Princesse de Lamballe was standing ready with a luxurious red dress for the dauphine's approval. Louise flashed back to the weird dream she had the other night of the old-fashioned women dressing her in the beautiful blue silk gown. There was something very similar about these two scenes. Maybe that crazy dream was a premonition of her time-traveling adventure to come!

"Excusez-moi." Louise was snapped back to her present reality as a tall older woman with a long hook nose and wearing a black feathered hat and a dark velvet cloak briskly pushed past her without a second look. The woman walked into the room, not bothering to shut the tall French doors behind her.

The whole process instantly stopped. The princess tilted her head to acknowledge the latecomer, who was leisurely taking off her cloak. The Princesse de Lamballe placed a dark poppy dress with a huge hoop skirt back on its padded hanger and handed it with a deferential nod to the older woman while the shivering dauphine, who was still almost naked and clearly very cold, looked on helplessly. Finally, after slowly and deliberately taking off her long brown leather riding gloves, the tall older woman helped the dauphine step into the unwieldy structured gown and carefully buttoned up the back. The Princesse de Lamballe then attached the long red silk train. It seemed completely over-the-top. No wonder she

started getting dressed for dinner in the middle of the afternoon. Depending on who decided to show up, this process could take all day!

"I put on my rouge and wash my hands in front of the whole world," the dauphine said softly. No one responded.

Louise suddenly felt sad. She didn't think it was possible to feel bad for a princess who had an awesome playhouse and lived in a real palace, but she couldn't imagine having to get dressed in front of an audience every day and not be able to even pick her own clothes from off the hanger. It was clear from the dauphine's mother's letter that she was forced by court tradition and etiquette to be completely helpless. Despite being in a room of people, she looked utterly alone.

"Can someone please close the door? The draft is ghastly," the sullen-faced princess ordered crossly.

The tall, inlaid ivory door slammed shut with a decisive bang, and Louise was left staring at the wrong side of a closed door. She reached up on her tiptoes and ran her hand over the gold carving on the upper panel, tracing the lines with her fingertips. Halfway through the pattern, she realized that it wasn't an abstract design—it was actually a monogram. She stepped back to gain some perspective and saw the letters *MA* drawn out in a fancy, elaborate script. That also sounded familiar. This bedroom belonged to an M.A.?

Versailles, palace, French words…whoa. This room in *Versailles* belonged to M.A.?!

There was only one lady she knew about who lived in Versailles. One very infamous historical figure whom her droll teacher Miss Morris was trying to tell her class about the other day. But it didn't make sense. This palace was so lovely and pristine, and the dauphine wasn't a grown-up woman she had been having tea with. She was probably just a few years older than Louise, no more than fourteen. How could the future Queen of France, the wife of King Louis XVI, be just a…teenager?

Ohmigod. It had to be…M.A.…*Marie Antoinette*. And she still had her head.

CHAPTER 17

Louise quickly backed away from the room where quite possibly the most famous woman in the history of France was standing, freezing cold in a slip and corset, waiting to be dressed by her royal court. With the door open!

She ran down the corridor toward her apartment in shock, her extravagantly heeled shoes echoing eerily throughout the deserted hallway. Could it really be her? Was Louise—or Gabrielle, rather—a lady-in-waiting in Marie Antoinette's inner circle? Though this Marie Antoinette wasn't like the one she'd imagined from Miss Morris's history lecture. She was just a girl, a young teen who had a cute puppy and liked to play hide-and-seek and have tea parties in her playhouse. She was someone who seemed in some ways to be just like Louise. Her mind immediately flashed back to the totally gruesome stories about the French Revolution and the violent end of the royal family that her otherwise dull teacher shocked the class with. This Versailles felt like the opposite of that, truly idyllic and beautiful. It didn't make any sense. It seemed like nothing bad could happen here.

As she turned the polished gold-plated doorknob to her new abode, Louise silently said a little prayer that there would not be an entourage waiting to dress Gabrielle. That looked extremely embarrassing. Although she could use a hand with the corset—it seemed pretty complicated. Now that she thought about it, how in the world was she supposed to fix her hair by herself? Some days she could barely manage a ponytail!

She cautiously entered the room, which was decorated with pink-and-gold floral wallpaper offset with white wainscoting, and found two servants in matching white, bright blue, and red uniforms (more regally colored and formal than the uniforms the maids wore at Petit Trianon) tidying up and waiting for Louise—er, Gabrielle—to return. They weren't alone. Her acquaintance, the older woman in the light brown long-sleeved dress from the garden tea party who had been giving her the stink eye all day, was also in the room...going through Gabrielle's closet! Was she being robbed?

"Excuse me?" Louise interrupted, clearing her throat. Adelaide spun around, apparently surprised to see her, as well, which was weird because she was in Gabrielle's room. "Are you looking for something?"

The chambermaids, who were busy steaming the train of a

gorgeous marigold satin gown across the suite, didn't seem to be paying any attention to their conversation. They turned briefly and gave Louise a curious look, then went back to decrinkling the crinoline. Some security guards they were.

Her intruder immediately shut the decoupaged armoire, regained her composure, and marched pointedly toward Louise. "*Excusez-moi*, I thought perhaps you borrowed my favorite silk evening gloves. I haven't been able to find them anywhere. I suppose I was mistaken," Adelaide replied defensively. Louise had a feeling by the way Adelaide spoke so quickly that silk evening gloves weren't really what she was looking for.

"I suppose you were," Louise answered tentatively. For some reason she had a nagging suspicion this woman was lying to her. But why? What would she expect to find in Gabrielle's closet?

"You should prepare yourself for the evening," Adelaide instructed, giving Louise a critical once-over. "It's almost sundown and you haven't even fixed your pouf yet."

Why did Louise feel like she was suddenly trapped in *Mean Girls*, Versailles edition? The haughty lady gave her a slight curtsey and quickly exited the room without glancing back.

CHAPTER 18

The moment her surprised visitor left the room, the servants rushed over to Louise with their arms full of finely hand-sewn garments and some medieval-looking beauty equipment. Before she realized what was happening, Louise was stripped of her lavender tea dress and wrapped up in a sheer white dressing gown like a fancy Parisian mummy. One of the maids, who was Louise's height but had a big matronly bosom, stood on a wooden step stool and went at her towering brown wig with a steaming-hot curling iron that must have been heated up over an open fire, as there were obviously no electrical cords at this time. The other maid, thin and gangly, reached up on her tiptoes and covered the whole mess with globs of greasy pomade and then dispensed a shower of white powder that smelled just like, and perhaps was, cake flour over the top of her head. Exactly how tall was this hairdo? Louise felt she must look a little bit like Marge Simpson after a cake-baking accident in an old-fashioned period dress. The women then studded the whole creation with at least a hundred diamond-tipped hairpins they had tucked in their apron pockets.

"*Aaaachoo!*" Louise let out an enormous sneeze, nearly scalding her forehead with the blistering-hot steel instrument.

The maid dispensing the sneezing powder then picked up a Costco-size golden pot of rouge from the vanity table and what appeared to be a horsehair makeup brush and drew what felt like two perfectly round circles on Louise's already powdered cheeks. She was beginning to feel certain that "less is more" must be a modern-day concept.

After the hair and makeup were complete, the maids left Louise alone for a moment to gather the appropriate garments and then gave her several more moments to check out her new fabulous bedroom. The room was sparsely furnished, with each ornately carved chair and foot stool upholstered in the same pink-and-gold brocade fabric as the walls and heavy curtains, which were drawn shut across the tall windows. There was a vanity table against the far wall that held a large, open, ebony jewelry box whose sparkly contents spilled out onto the glass top and a dome-shape canopy bed on a low platform that was draped in matching tapestry fabric.

Hanging above the mantelpiece was an ornately framed oil

painting of a woman sitting at a table with her hands crossed. The woman was posing naturally in a white muslin dress with a deep V-neck ruffled bodice, smiling sweetly for the artist. She wore a floppy straw hat with a blue ribbon and wildflowers attached to the brim, which partially covered her deep chestnut-colored hair that fell in wild, loose waves around her face. Her flawless, milky complexion was offset by her remarkable violet-tinged eyes (and these were definitely the days before colored contact lenses). This must have been Gabrielle! She was psyched; if this portrait was any indication, Louise was now undeniably, totally gorgeous.

Before she had time to bask in her newfound beauty, the two stylists came at her with the odious corset. If Louise felt like she had been physically restricted dressing up as Miss Alice Baxter in 1912 on board the *Titanic*, this was a whole new and unfortunate level of discomfort. It seemed that the farther back she traveled in history, the more pained and restricted women were. Literally. By the time the maids had laced the back of the whale-bone corset up over her thin chemise (yes, it was actually made of whale bones—she asked), Louise was seeing stars, and not in a good way. They then tied something that looked like a life preserver around her that extended Louise to just about double her girth so that the pleats of the dress could fall properly. Why they squeezed her in just to ultimately give her a caboose that would make Kim Kardashian look teeny was beyond her.

"I...I can't breathe...." she gasped. She thought there was a very real possibility that she was going to faint right there on the needlepoint carpet. To Louise's pain and bafflement, the two uniformed women tried rather unsuccessfully to stifle a giggle. As though not taking in enough oxygen and possibly passing out for the sake of an hourglass figure was some sort of joke.

If there was any payoff for all that torture, though, then it most definitely came in the form of the most fabulous marigold-colored evening dress Louise had ever laid eyes on. The gown was composed of three separate pieces of a fine orange silk: a structured bodice, a ginormous hoop skirt, and a long sweeping train. The dress was decorated with gathered bands of gold silk twisted backward and forward over the bodice. The sleeve ruffles were covered with sprigs of tiny silk-and-taffeta flowers with little jade-colored leaves and petals, all clearly hand-stitched.

The main part of the dress was slowly and dramatically lowered down over Louise's corseted body like a stage curtain on opening night. As she ran her fingers over the luxurious fabric and intricate detailing, all her twelve-year-old insecurities that far too frequently ran through her head like an evil mantra—too skinny, too flat-chested, too short, too quirky—

were wiped clean. She was being given a fresh start. For the first time since her experience as Miss Baxter, Louise felt like a true diva. She glanced up at the larger-than-life-size framed portrait of Gabrielle looking down over her and felt protected by and connected to this total stranger. For some reason she had been chosen for this.

Now she was ready to find the party.

CHAPTER 19

After three failed attempts at exiting the room, Louise awkwardly discovered that she had to turn herself sideways in order to pass through the doorway with her silk bustle intact. She once again heard the muffled giggles of her two chambermaids and had a feeling that she might be in for a long night.

The vast arched hallway was now crowded with a buzzing swarm of hundreds of formally attired guests, all dressed up in different color variations of Louise's elaborate fancy outfit. The sun was setting and the dusky orange light lazily filtered in through the tall paned windows. A dazzling row of sparkly glass chandeliers suspended on red velvet-covered chains were now aglow with hundreds of dripping waxy candles.

The men wore dark cropped britches that reached their knees, met by bright white silk socks. They all had knee-length black- or navy-tailed silk coats worn over matching vests with detailed embroidery down the breast, frilly linen shirts, and powdered hair or perhaps wigs that were pulled back in ponytails with dark silk bows. Their leather shoes had stacked heels and were fastened with buckles or ribbons. But the men looked almost insignificant next to their female companions, whose rich purple, sapphire blue, or ruby red jewel-toned bubble skirts and extravagant hairstyles took up much of the space in the magnificent hall.

Louise let herself blend into the current of chattering people. Someone had to know where they were going. She felt her silver embroidered shoe catch on the train of the woman in front of her, who snapped around to give her a nasty look.

"Do watch where you are walking," she trilled in a huff. This was going to be a challenge, as Louise generally had enough problems not tripping in her normal life without having to worry about stepping on the vast silk tails that all the women seemed to be dragging behind them.

"My dear Gabrielle," a tinkling voice called from behind her as a pink satin-gloved arm gracefully linked through hers. She turned to see the Princesse de Lamballe smiling gently back with her sweet watery blue eyes. She had changed into a dusky rose-colored gown with matching dyed lace trim delicately peeking out of the structured bodice and a lone strand of ivory pearls looped twice around her neck. Jeweled barrettes held up her teased blonde hair with a few perfectly placed curls framing her heart-shaped face. She looked beautiful.

"Isn't it a lovely evening?" she asked, as though it were just a typical night in Versailles.

"Yes, it is," Louise replied, not able to mask the gigantic smile that must have been plastered on her face. She was trying, unsuccessfully, to not seem too excited about what, to this girl, was just another fancy dinner. This was sooo much more than a lovely evening, Louise thought as she looked around at what appeared to be foreign dignitaries and European society ladies graciously mingling as they made their way down the corridor. Some of these people probably had whole chapters devoted to them in her history books! Now if only she could persuade one of them to write her term paper for her...

"You look marvelous; you always do, of course!" the Princesse de Lamballe exclaimed. And, for once, Louise believed it.

The girls walked arm and arm into what must have been the royal dining hall, which was now packed with spectators. "Who are all these people?" Louise couldn't help but ask.

"Why, mostly they live here, but Versailles is open to everyone, as you know," the princess answered, seemingly shocked that Louise—or Gabrielle, rather—was naïve to the workings of the palace. "Of course they must have a hat and a sword to be admitted."

"Really?" Louise asked, surprised. "I mean, of course. I knew that." She thought a palace was supposed to be a private, exclusive space. It seemed like half the people in France must be here. She couldn't imagine thousands of people making their home in the White House or it being open to any tourist who happened to show up with the required hat and sword. Particularly the sword part.

The dining room was rather strange, too. It was a grand room with a shiny waxed parquet floor, deep red walls, and a gold stucco ceiling inlaid with masterly painted oil murals, and it seemed as though it was a Versailles tradition that the royal court ate their supper in public. At the far side of the room, a dining table covered in a long white cloth was set up with two ornate candelabras, silver covered platters, and soup terrines. Marie Antoinette and the portly and unattractive Louis XVI, whom Louise recognized from earlier that afternoon, sat side by side in two matching armchairs looking out toward the room. A semicircle of maroon velvet stools trimmed with golden tassels arced the other side of the table and were occupied by ladies of the court. The rest of the audience stood behind a few feet away.

In her old life, Louise would be self-conscious eating a toasted sesame bagel at a crowded lunch table. She couldn't imagine sitting on a platform and cutting up her vegetables while everyone gawked. Maybe that was why Marie Antoinette was so skinny. Maybe it made her really uncomfortable to eat in front of all those people.

Louise watched as Louis, grease dribbling down his chin,

greedily gnawed on a chicken leg while the dauphine, as Louise remembered she was called, sat there quietly, occasionally taking a tiny teaspoonful of consommé with her white-gloved hand. Her napkin remained neatly folded next to her plate. In contrast, Louis paused only long enough to pop a whole hard-boiled egg in his mouth or to take a gulp of red wine that dribbled down his chin from the goblet held out to him by another member of the royal court. It seemed like he didn't even notice that a few feet away a crowd of people were gawking and staring at him. Did these people ever get a moment of privacy? Or was privacy a modern concept as well? Louise didn't think the president and first lady would be cool with this invasive setup.

There was a whole gaggle of ladies in colorful satin gowns with big bustles waiting as still as marble statues to pass Marie Antoinette a new fork or glass of water if she so desired, which she rarely did. Louise noticed the married couple barely said a word to each other during the whole meal. They just stared straight ahead as though they were mannequins in a display window at Bloomingdale's or some fancy department store as the audience watched, captivated.

The Princesse de Lamballe was standing next to Louise, gazing admiringly at Marie Antoinette as she took a tiny, mouselike nibble of a spring green asparagus spear. This was too weird. Louise needed some fresh air.

"We should take our places, shan't we?" the princess asked, gesturing to two empty seats directly in front of the dauphine.

Looking at Marie Antoinette's best friend's wide, innocent blue eyes, Louise had a quick horrifying flashback to Miss Morris lecturing about how the Princesse de Lamballe would ultimately find her head on a pike paraded through the streets of France. *The poor Princesse de Lamballe's detached head was first taken to a hairdresser, ensuring that everyone, particularly Marie Antoinette, would recognize her,* she heard her teacher state simply in a monotone.

"I'm going out to the garden," Louise whispered back in a shaky voice. The princess excused herself and walked over to an empty stool and, with perfect posture, carefully lowered herself, arranging her billowing dusky pink satin skirts around her.

Louise started trembling. This simply couldn't be. The Princesse de Lamballe was basically just a teenager trying to please the popular girl in school. She suddenly realized with a shudder that if Gabrielle was one of Marie Antoinette's close friends, then maybe she would soon be in danger of finding her head on a stake, too!

Louise *definitely* wanted to get back home to her life in Connecticut before she found out if that was true and it was too late. If only she had done her school reading—maybe she could have remembered when, exactly, the French Revolution took place. Why didn't she know by now to pay attention dur-ing Miss Morris's boring but obviously critically important and now relevant-to-her-life history lectures?!

This seemed to be a very dramatic way to learn her lessons. She needed to figure out a plan and clear her head...while she still had one.

CHAPTER 20

Louise quickly walked out of the lit-up palace, skipped down the low white steps glimmering in the deep red early evening light, and headed into the garden. The sun had almost set and the usually populated paths were nearly empty. She reached up to twirl her hair, something she instinctively did when she got nervous or tired, or just needed to think, and was reminded that she now had a coarse twelve-inch-high powdered Brillo pad attached to the top of her head. *Gross.*

She turned down a narrow path, the warm rays scattering across the white pebbles, which made a satisfying crunching sound under her heels, and abruptly found herself face-to-face with her new gardener crush. Still in his uniform except for his three-cornered hat, which was on the grass by his black leather boots, he was leaning casually against a wide tree trunk and laughing at a newspaper he was intently looking at.

When he smiled, his coffee-colored brown eyes gleamed. She could make out a cute dimple in his left cheek.

"What are you reading?" Louise asked with a smile after she'd regained her composure. She had an annoying tendency to get weird and shy around cute guys, so she thought back to that gorgeous painting of Gabrielle and was given a jolt of confidence. It was who she was right now. At least on the outside. She made a swipe for the paper he was holding.

"No...nothing!" he stuttered, quickly hiding the sheet of newsprint behind his back.

"What's so funny?" Louise asked again, now just curious, as it seemed the flirting part wasn't going so well.

"Nothing, mademoiselle," he repeated as he lowered his flushed, tan face, still refusing to make eye contact.

Then Louise realized...he was scared of her? Well, not her, but Gabrielle. And whatever she represented. How could she hint to him she really wasn't that woman without actually exposing the truth?

"I'm not like the others," she finally said more vaguely. "You can trust me." He didn't say anything. The silence was deafening. "What's your name?" She was hoping to get anything out of him.

"*Je m'appelle* Pierre," he replied quietly.

"I'm...Gabrielle," she answered, wishing for the first time on this crazy voyage that she could just be Louise again. She had a weird feeling this Pierre would actually like her more as herself.

When he glanced up, Louise noticed his brown eyes had subtle flecks of green, and he nervously looked directly at her for the very first time. She felt her face start to turn hot and blotchy. Embarrassed, she did the only ridiculous thing she could think of and snatched the paper out of his hands.

Louise opened up the now crumpled news sheet and discovered a crude black-and-white illustration that bore a striking resemblance to Marie Antoinette. In the drawing the dauphine was done up in clownlike makeup and an exaggeratedly tall hairstyle with a ship sticking out of it. The caption simply read MADAME DEFICIT. What did that mean? Louise could tell it wasn't meant to be very nice, like a nasty note being passed around during math class behind someone's back. She had a feeling if Marie Antoinette saw this, the gardener would be fired, or worse....

No wonder he was scared of her! It seemed as though Gabrielle was one of the princess's closest confidantes. Why would he be reading something like this? Maybe the newspaper was like *In Touch Weekly* or *Us Weekly* of eighteenth-century France.

"I don't know if I get it," she admitted finally. The gardener breathed an audible sigh of relief. "But I want to." Pierre tensed up again. "Please, trust me," she pleaded. "What is it like outside the palace? Are the French people happy?" She had a feeling from her history class she already knew the answer to that question.

"Happy?" he asked, confused, as though the concept of happiness was a modern-day construct.

"Are they…content?" Louise asked again. "Please tell me the truth."

Pierre paused, tight-lipped, unsure how to respond. "They are suffering. There is not enough food. People are starving," he replied softly but with intense emotion. "There are frequent revolts over the cost of grain. But please do not say anything about this. I would lose my job, and I need my salary to support the rest of my family."

Whoa, this guy, maybe a few years older than Louise, was supporting his family and not the other way around? She suddenly missed her parents and couldn't help but feel a little guilty right then about the spoiled way she'd acted during her last few days at home.

"I'm sorry. I wish I could help," she said, truly meaning it. "And maybe I can. Marie Antoinette needs to know what's going on outside of Versailles. She's isolated here. Maybe if she understood, she would get the king to help…." Louise inadvertently placed her hand on his. She felt a small electric jolt course through her body and quickly pulled her hand away. He jumped slightly.

144

Before she could examine and reflect on the intensity of the charged moment, Pierre hastily grabbed back the paper, scooped up his hat, and took off running through the freshly trimmed hedges without even a quick glance back or an *au revoir.* Apparently he had been shocked, too, but clearly not in a good way.

CHAPTER 21

Deep in thought, Louise went back up the ever-darkening path toward Versailles. The illuminated palace was humming with energy. Maybe she could use Gabrielle's influence with Marie Antoinette to help the French people and possibly avoid the bloody revolution. *But how?*

From the terrace she could hear the buzz of conversation mingled with classical harpsichord music and laughter. Taking a deep breath, or one as deep as possible while wearing a corset, she said a silent prayer that she'd be able to pull this one off. She was starting to feel less like Gabrielle by the minute.

The party was the most decadent and debaucherous affair Louise had witnessed in her twelve years. Even the first-class dining room on the *Titanic* seemed uptight in comparison. Her mom would most definitely *not* approve, she thought as she politely refused a crystal glass of champagne that was immediately offered to her as she walked in through the tall, arched, glass-paned door.

Uniformed card dealers were presiding over an intense hand; there were roulette wheels, poker chips, and dice games in play. The triumphant shouts of the winners were almost drowned out by an orchestra that was playing in the far corner of the salon. A waiter poured frothy champagne over a pyramid of crystal glasses in the center of the long dining table. The tabletop was also piled high with sweets and cakes and a rainbow of dainty, pastel, iced pastries that guests greedily grabbed at with their fingers, smearing frosting on the expensive-looking upholstery and grinding crumbs into the jewel-toned carpets with the high heels of their diamond-buckled or shiny, tasseled shoes. *Ohmigod*—her mother would die to see such well-dressed adults behaving like unsupervised toddlers.

Louise immediately spotted Marie Antoinette, glowing and looking fabulous in a new ivory-and-gold dress (How many times a day did this girl change her outfits? She counted three wardrobe changes so far!), and flirting and giggling like any high school–age girl at a party. She looked like a natural hostess, gliding her way around the room as though on ice skates, her posture perfect and her head tilted up in such a way that there was no doubt this was *her* party. She paused to

sample a bite-size cake as she roamed around with delight, naturally making everyone feel welcome. Marie Antoinette was definitely in her element now—the "It" girl of eighteenth-century France.

It seemed like her husband was far less social. Instead of dancing or gambling, Louis XVI was sitting at a table of somber-looking men and showing off some sort of steel lock-and-key contraption that he was nervously toying with.

"He's obsessed with those locks." Louise jumped. She hadn't noticed that Adelaide was now standing next to her. "The dauphine finds the whole thing quite boring, and I don't blame her. Do you?"

Louise shook her head. The whole scene still felt quite surreal.

"Let us sit, shall we? These shoes are getting most constricting." The woman sighed as she pulled out a red upholstered dining chair, and they sat at the table among a group of party guests.

"Who is that lady?" Louise asked, discreetly pointing at a raven-haired woman in a particularly low-cut scarlet gown practically dripping with diamonds and rubies. She was seductively perched on the arm of a high-back chair with a live green-and-blue parrot on her arm. The regally dressed older man sitting in the chair held up a pair of dice, and she blew them a kiss before he threw them out on the green felt-top gaming table. Everyone cheered as they raked in the chips. "Great roll, Your Highness!"

"Ha," Adelaide snorted. "That's Madame du Barry, of course."

"Du what?" Louise asked, confused. Then she remembered to keep her poise.

"Du Barry. King Louis XV's mistress," a woman seated nearby finished with a raised eyebrow. "Did you not know? I personally find the whole affair quite offensive."

"Seriously?" Louise asked again, trying to figure out exactly what that meant. Like his girlfriend but not really? "I mean, of course I did. She just looks different with that bird on her arm or something...."

Madame du Barry was whispering in the king's ear and tickling his cheek with a long black ostrich feather. The rest of the people at the table were either pretending nothing was happening or blatantly gossiping about it as Louise and these women were. It was superweird. Louise was convinced Madame du Barry had shot her and Adelaide a dirty look, realizing they must have been staring. *Oops.*

Before visiting Versailles, Louise had imagined that in a royal court everyone would be very uptight and respectful. She was shocked to discover her nightly dinners at home with her parents were more formal than in this palace. Red wine was spilled in blotchy pools all over the tablecloth. Poker chips and playing cards were dropped haphazardly, and fluffy cats were everywhere, eating off half-eaten dinner plates around the table. She lifted her arm to discover it was resting in a pile of greasy crumbs. Maybe this was where the no-elbows-on-the-table rule first originated, she thought as she brushed off the oily debris, which left a wet stain on her emerald satin sleeve. Yuck. Adelaide laughed at Louise's disgusted expression.

Marie Antoinette was only a few years older than Louise, and yet, in this moment it felt like decades. She wished they were back at Petit Trianon playing hide-and-seek. Or that she was back in Connecticut picking out a playlist for Brooke's thirteenth birthday party.

She picked up an oversized puffy yellow macaroon from the top tier of a display of sherbet-tone cookies and took a huge bite, breaking the delicate shell and getting a mouthful of tangy lemon-flavored cream. Tomorrow would be the day when she would confront Marie Antoinette and try to help Pierre and the rest of the French people, she decided as she took another heavenly bite. Louise wondered if she would be carrying ten extra pounds back with her to Connecticut or if these stayed in the past. She'd have to ask Marla and Glenda about that one and hope for the best. These French pastries were way too good to miss, and they were impossible to— they were everywhere. Huge, artfully arranged towers of pastel-colored sweets covered all the available tabletops,

adjoined by platters of wild strawberries with clotted cream. Versailles was not the kind of place you'd want to be if you were contemplating a diet.

"Oh, you must try this one," Louise urged Adelaide, picking up an oozing pink cream-filled raspberry cookie despite the fact that her whalebone corset was strongly urging her otherwise.

"Why, thank you." A smooth ivory-colored hand plucked the sweet from Louise's outstretched palm. Marie Antoinette took a tiny bite of the pastry.

"Now, isn't this simply a marvelous party?" she asked with a wink. "I do believe the Swedes are enjoying themselves. Let's go outside for the fireworks. The night is only just beginning!"

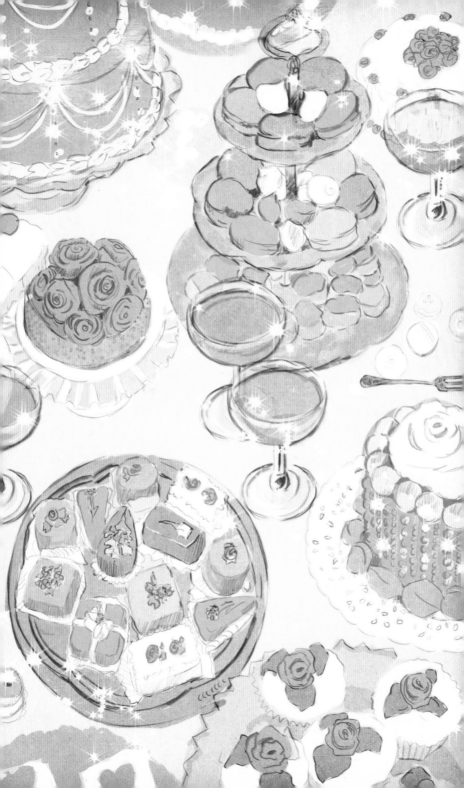

CHAPTER 22

Marie Antoinette led Louise, Adelaide, and a select group of her closest friends out onto the vast, manicured lawn, laughing as she dragged her pearly white silk train through the dirt and dewy grass. Louise realized that it didn't matter if this gown got ruined. There would always be a new, more fabulous dress waiting for her in the morning.

"Let's play a game!" Marie Antoinette decided, clapping her hands excitedly. "Everyone will hide, and Count Fersen and I will find you," she decided, pointing to a tall, handsome blond man dressed in a military uniform. "I'll count to ten. *Un, deux, trois…*"

Louise smiled. She and Brooke used to play this game all the time when they were younger. The Lamberts' house was loaded with lots of nooks and deceptively deep closets. The women kicked off their high-heeled shoes, and everyone scattered in different directions. Louise took off running toward the rose garden, feeling free and happy in that moment to act like a kid again. Racing in her stockinged feet through the moist grass, she never wanted to go back to her old life where she had to turn thirteen and change somehow. Where she found it almost impossible to run through the grass without thinking about how childlike that would look.

Then she saw him and stopped. Pierre was wandering through the rosebushes, whistling some song she didn't recognize and looking up at the sky, lost in his own thoughts. He looked startled at first and then almost seemed to smile.

"*Bonsoir*," he said, taking off his hat in a chivalrous gesture.

"Good evening," Louise responded shyly. "Nice to see you again. The garden looks lovely."

"*Merci.*" He nodded, brushing a stray piece of wavy brown hair off his forehead and looking genuinely pleased by the compliment. "My apologies for running off earlier."

"It's okay. I thought it was something I said." She tried to discreetly adjust the twisted bustle of her skirt.

"No, of course not," he quickly answered.

"I'd like to hear more about your family. What are they like?" Louise felt a little guilty that she had let herself get so distracted earlier by some fancy cookies.

"My father is a cobbler. My mother does her best to take care of my brothers and sisters; there are six of us, but it has been tough as of late. It seems like there is not enough of anything to go around for most people. Although here you would never know it."

"I know; Versailles is like a dream. My family is having some trouble with money right now, too," Louise said, thinking of her dad's job, although she had a feeling that it was a different level of financial trouble from what Pierre was experiencing.

"Thank you. You are very easy to speak with. I did not think you would be like this."

"Umm, thanks?" she replied, not sure if that was a compliment.

Louise looked down at her shimmery dress and felt a mixture of confidence and sadness. She wasn't herself right now. This felt all so surreal. Maybe too surreal. She was playing the role of a fancy royal court girl, which was fun, but she also wanted it to seem like her real life. In a weird way she kind of wanted something really awkward and embarrassing to happen just so she'd be able to recognize herself and know that she hadn't created this whole fabulous scenario in her head. She didn't have to wait for long.

"It is a beautiful evening, is it not?" Pierre looked down into her eyes and leaned closer as though he were about to kiss her, but before anything could actually happen, they were startled by something that sounded like gunfire going off all around them. *Ohmigod.* Had the revolution started already?!

"Duck!" Louise screamed, diving to the ground.

159

She looked up through her fingers to see a colorful shower of cascading fireworks exploding in the sky above them. Louise awkwardly got up from the grass and dusted off her gown. Pierre began to retreat, the loud blasts snapping him back to reality.

Typical. Finally, Louise's life was like a movie, a really good foreign movie, but a sudden fireworks display had ruined her chance at her first kiss! She should know better than to wish for a more "real" experience. She couldn't help but wonder where Todd was at that moment.

But still, Louise *almost* had her first kiss with a totally hot French boy. She was sure of it. No one would believe that at Fairview and she didn't quite believe it herself. Ummm, he's really cute, French, from the olden times. No, you probably haven't run into him before. Yeah, it's kind of a long-distance thing. Like really long distance, pre-Skype. Like 250 years.

The last burst of royal-blue-and-white sparkly light trailed down in the sky, and the garden was quiet again. "Wait, did you hear that?" Pierre asked, putting his hand on her arm, which set off a million butterflies in Louise's stomach.

"Hear what?" There was a loud swishing sound coming from the hedges. "Okay, I heard it that time," she agreed.

"Do you think they're coming after us? Do you think they know about us?" Pierre whispered loudly, nervously wiping his hands on his uniform. He was clearly starting to panic. About what, she wasn't sure.

"Know about us?" Louise whispered back, perplexed. Was he that embarrassed to be seen with her?

The rustling noise was getting closer; someone or something was moving quickly toward them.

"We need to hide," Pierre grabbed Louise's hand and they ducked behind a tall rosebush. *Ouch.* With thorns and all.

The crunching of leaves turned into a familiar high-pitched giggling.

"Marie Antoinette?" Louise whispered quietly in surprise to Pierre.

She stared with her mouth dropped open in shock as the dauphine and the handsome uniformed man from the hide-and-seek game, Count Fersen, who was most definitely about ten years younger and one million times cuter than Louis, ran by them holding hands, deeper into the garden. *Ohmygawd.* Did she really just see that?

As soon as they passed, Louise burst into nervous, relieved laughter.

"I guess we picked a popular meeting space. Think we'll find anyone else in the hedges?" Louise joked, completely covered in rosebushes.

"I don't know, but I must leave." Pierre's eyes nervously

darted around as though someone were going to jump out of the shadows. Louise couldn't help but feel a little hurt and confused by the strange way he was acting.

"*Merci*," he said quietly with his thick eyelashes lowered to the ground. Without another word he ran off for the second time that day into the pitch-black night, leaving Louise standing alone, shivering in a thorny rosebush.

CHAPTER 23

Louise was abruptly awoken by a sharp rapping on her bedroom door. Startled, she lifted her powder pink silk sleeping mask and groggily opened one eye. How she had managed to finally fall asleep after replaying the night over and over on her mind's movie screen and with her neck uncomfortably crooked up on three down pillows to support her giant pile of hair was beyond her. Today she was definitely going to have a bit of a crick, to say the least.

Marie Antoinette whisked into the room, looking fresh and dewy in a new key lime green dress, drawing open the heavy tapestry drapes and letting in a sharp stream of sunlight.

"My dear heart, Gabrielle," she sang. Someone was in a good mood. Louise had a flashback to a giggling Marie Antoinette running through the moonlit gardens with that cute Swedish officer who was definitely not her doughy,

awkward husband and had a little idea of why this might be. "Have you forgotten? Today we go to Paris. We must visit Rose Bertin's shop to purchase some new frocks. You promised!"

She did? *Umm, okay!*

Paris? Shopping? That was more than enough to get Louise to forget about her sore neck and jump down from the huge platform canopy bed. It seemed like she was actually going to Paris after all! She wondered if she was living in a BLV (Before Louis Vuitton) era. She hoped not and was pretty sure the original Louis Vuitton founded the company in the mid-1800s. How cool would it be to actually own one of the original LV monogrammed steamer trunks! Now if only she could remember the dates of the French Revolution with such clarity then she'd be getting a much better grade in history class.

"My darling mother sent me another love letter today from Austria," Marie Antoinette said, pulling out a folded sheet of cream-colored paper from the bodice of her dress. May I read you a snippet?"

My Dearest Daughter,
It's not your beauty, which frankly is not very great. Nor your talents, nor your brilliance (you know perfectly well that you have neither).

The dauphine paused. "Shall I go on?"

There was a moment of uncomfortable silence. "I'm sorry," Louise shook her head in disbelief. She didn't know what else to say. She couldn't imagine getting a letter like that from her mother and wanted to distract her new friend from this awful note, so she gave her a reassuring squeeze then smiled. "Forget this for now. Let's go shopping!" Louise would try to talk to the dauphine about Pierre's family and everything else when they got back from the trip to Paris. This no longer seemed like the appropriate moment to bring it up.

"It's fine. I know she is simply worried about securing the alliance between our two countries, which of course won't be assured until I have our first child." A dark flicker of emotion quickly passed over Marie Antoinette's face and in an instant her happy disposition reappeared like the sun after a brief afternoon shower. "Not even she can ruin a glorious day as today! I will wait for you in the north garden by the Neptune basin. Please be hasty, my sweet, the carriage is ready."

As if they were waiting in the wings for their stage cue, Gabrielle's two personal maids, one still stout and one still tall, marched purposefully into the bedroom with their arms full of clothing and corsets to prepare Louise for her first journey to Paris.

CHAPTER 24

Even though the interior of the horse-drawn carriage was superluxurious like everything else Marie Antoinette owned, with plush peacock blue velvet seats and gold detailing, the ride was still a bumpy and loud ordeal with the wheels getting caught in the uneven countryside and rocking the two girls to and fro like a tossing ship on an angry sea. Marie Antoinette had to partially open the carriage window and slightly angle her head out so that the top of her two-foot-high pouf wouldn't get smashed into the roof of the coach. To divert herself from the nauseating ride, Louise had decided to busy herself with her favorite distraction—fashion.

"When was the last time Rose Bertin made you a new gown?" she asked, suddenly remembering Rose Bertin was the same designer Marla and Glenda were talking about at the sale. The same woman who had designed Louise's glorious blue dress . . . and she was about to meet her . . . in person!

"Yesterday, I suppose," Marie Antoinette answered distractedly. "She visits me twice a week with new ideas and fabrics and sketches. I would spend all day with her if I could. Rose is far more interesting than any of the dull dignitaries the king insists I entertain."

"That sounds amazing," Louise sighed, realizing she may have found the one person more obsessed with fashion than herself. "I mean, I know, isn't it amazing?"

"It is, isn't it?" Marie Antoinette marveled, turning her full attention to Louise. "All of you women in my court may only purchase your frocks from her from now on. It won't be long before Paris becomes the epicenter of fashion, and Rose and I will be the reason why. The rest of Europe will look toward us to see what is couture."

So this is when Paris became *the* place for haute couture. And Louise was here to see the beginning of it all! "I believe you're right about that epicenter stuff," she remarked enthusiastically. "How did you discover Rose?" Louise momentarily forgot to keep up the Gabrielle act.

"I met her through the Princesse de Lamballe, of course. And I recognized her talent immediately. She has been working closely with me ever since, as you know, my dear."

They drove through miles of heavily wooded landscape and unspoiled rolling hills spotted with the occasional thatched-roof cottage. It all started to blur together until they finally felt the smooth cobblestone under the coach wheels. Louise was actually in Paris!

"Stop here," Marie Antoinette ordered the driver, rapping sharply on the carriage window with her ginormous canary yellow diamond ring. "After that long journey, a small walk will do us some good. Don't you think, Gabrielle?"

Louise nodded mutely. She was doing her best not to be carsick or horse-drawn-carriage sick. A little Dramamine like her mother sometimes gave her on particularly long car rides would have been nice.

When the two fancily dressed girls were helped down from their luxurious carriage, the first thing that hit Louise was the stench. The air smelled pungent and thick, like rotten food mixed with sweat and body odor. To keep from gagging, she had to cover her mouth with her perfumed handkerchief (which now seemed like a very wise accessory to have tucked into her skirts). Why did this place smell so...disgusting?

The second was the noise. Street vendors selling bread, brooms, and oysters were shouting, hawking their wares, and trying to compete with the clatter of horse-drawn carriages barreling down the crowded cobblestone streets.

"Shoe shine, get your shoe shine here!" a man with a patched-up overcoat carrying a brush and kit yelled at the top of his lungs on the other side of the narrow lane. Louise thought for a moment about Pierre's family and suddenly understood why he would be scared to lose his gardening job at the palace. Life outside the tall iron-and-gold gates looked hard.

Paris was not at all what she had expected, to say the least. From every French movie Louise saw, the city was supposed to be postcard beautiful and utterly romantic. She thought the charming streets were going to be filled with the most fashionably dressed people on the planet, walking around with Hermès scarves knotted effortlessly around their necks, baguettes popping out of their classic Birkin bags, and drinking little coffees at elegant cafés. What she was quickly learning was that the Paris of the past was a totally different, far less cinematic story.

Her satin high-heeled slipper got caught in a rut and Louise had to grab on to Marie Antoinette so that she didn't totally wipe out on the cobblestone street, which was slick with grime, and fall into the pungent open sewer running alongside it. Piles of garbage were rotting on every street corner. Tiny children with wide eyes, dressed in raggedy clothing, were huddled in the corners, hands outstretched, begging for coins or a piece of bread. Louise noticed that the attendants walking with them made sure none of the children got too close. It seemed as though they were doing their best to keep the poverty at the periphery of Marie Antoinette's vision, and she herself didn't seem to want to see what wasn't directly in front of her.

Louise began fumbling for her change purse, which was tucked into the lining of her heavy maroon cloak, saddened and unprepared to see so much suffering after being isolated in the excess and riches of life at Versailles.

"Stop," the burly attendant ordered. "As you are aware, if you give them anything we will be mobbed. Keep walking and smile. Do as the dauphine does." Scolded, Louise lowered her head and continued on past the drab stone houses colored gray with soot.

"When will you give us an heir to the throne?" an angry voice called from the crowd. Louise looked over at Marie Antoinette, who flinched at the question, or rather, the demand. An heir? The people expected her to have a son. She was barely a few years older than Louise and she was already getting yelled at for not having a baby?!

It made Louise sad to see the blatant suffering of the Parisians but also to see this young girl with the weight and responsibility of a nation on her delicate shoulders. Though the dauphine seemed to recover instantly. She readjusted her beautiful cobalt blue velvet wrap and walked proudly through the dirty Parisian streets toward Rose Bertin's shop.

They soon arrived at Rue Saint-Honoré. The boutique, which Marie Antoinette told her was known as Au Grand Mogol, was impossible to miss, as there were several large showcase windows displaying all the beautiful dresses and jewelry and lace shawls that evidently made the Rose Bertin brand famous. The juxtaposition of this fancy store and the utter poverty she had just witnessed a few streets away baffled Louise. A uniformed doorman quickly led them inside the boutique, collecting their cloaks with a dramatic flourish.

Marie Antoinette let out a small sigh and Louise could tell she was immediately soothed by the luxurious dresses and familiar atmosphere. The overpowering fishy smell of trash was instantly transformed into the sweet scents of talcum powder mixed with floral perfume. It actually smelled a lot like Versailles.

"My dear dauphine, so lovely for you to make the trip to Paris to visit my humble atelier," Rose announced with a slight deferential curtsey. "And it's wonderful to see you again, too, Duchesse de Polignac. I do hope the journey wasn't too taxing."

Louise looked around and raised her eyebrows at the elaborate decor. *Humble atelier?* The shop reminded her of a dressing room back at the palace with tall vaulted ceilings, pink-and-gold silk brocade-upholstered stools and love seats positioned underneath richly painted landscapes in ornate frames, and round marble tables topped with tall vases of white lilies. A yard of red silk was draped over a mannequin fitted with a big bustle, as though Rose was interrupted in the midst of sewing together her latest creation. There was definitely

nothing humble about this place. Compared with the Paris she had just walked through, the opulence of this shop made her a little queasy.

Rose Bertin, the godmother of French couture, turned out to be a stout woman with a rough, ruddy complexion. She looked more like she should be working on a farm—the opposite image of her refined boutique and overtly feminine dresses. She was much older and coarser than Louise had expected. Rose had several assistants working for her in the shop, who all did a slight curtsey when Marie Antoinette and Gabrielle walked in. They were young, beautiful, and wearing sophisticated pink uniforms. The assistants seemed to exemplify the Rose Bertin brand that, at least physically, Rose herself did not.

"I love Paris. One simply must escape Versailles every so often and reconnect with the city and the people," Marie Antoinette gushed as she picked up a sapphire-jeweled hair-comb from a velvet box and stuck it into her platinum blonde pouf.

Louise didn't think rushing through a mob of angry and hungry Parisians and directly into a fancy boutique consti-tuted reconnecting with the people, but she wasn't going to say anything to her now. She also didn't understand how this young royal could be so oblivious to the blatant suffering of the average French person. Maybe if Louise could somehow explain things to her and tell her that she needed to take their situation as seriously as she took picking out a new dress, then she, or rather Gabrielle, could help change history.

"We had a visit yesterday from the lovely Mademoiselle de Mirecourt," Rose Bertin remarked as she gathered some baubles and sparkly accessories from around the shop to show to the dauphine.

"Oh, yes, and what did she purchase?" Marie Antoinette asked with a raised eyebrow.

"I am making her a turquoise lévite," Rose Bertin announced, holding up a fluttery, sheer, blue-green gown. "It's similar to the one you ordered last month."

"Very good," Marie Antoinette answered, apparently relieved she wore the design first.

"You must have a look at this fabulous chenille fabric. You are the first to see it, of course. I think that with your milky complexion this will look simply marvelous on you," Rose sang confidently as an assistant pulled out a roll of gauzy soft yellow hidden underneath the long mahogany counter, the color of the buttercups in Marie Antoinette's vast garden.

"That's divine; do you have ribbon trim?" she asked, clapping her hands in excitement.

"Of course." Another stylishly dressed assistant climbed up on a wooden step stool and pulled down a thick spool of matching yellow silk ribbon from the upper shelf.

"I'd like one right away. Would you, Gabrielle?" Marie Antoinette asked, turning toward Louise.

"Yes, please." Louise immediately replied. She wasn't one to turn down a free couture dress.

"Perhaps you would prefer the puce color?" Rose Bertin quickly interjected, signaling to a different assistant to get down another roll of muted pinkish-brown fabric.

"But I like this one," Louise insisted, admiring the yellow silk. The other was kind of... blah.

"My dear, puce is more your color, correct?" Rose asked curtly. "I am always right about these things—you must trust me." She gave Louise a searing look. Maybe yellow was *really* not Gabrielle's color? Louise noticed the assistants shooting subtle but nervous glances at one another. Then she realized she wasn't supposed to wear the same thing as the dauphine. That must have been the expected court protocol.

"I suppose you're right. The other one is beautiful, too," Louise agreed quickly, touching the silky spool of puce-colored fabric.

Marie Antoinette smiled. "I was hoping you would choose that one. I've always loved to see you in puce."

CHAPTER 25

"Why do you shop so much?" Louise couldn't help but wonder aloud on the long and bumpy carriage ride back to Versailles. The plushly upholstered compartment was completely packed with their beautifully wrapped parcels. The two girls were wedged between the boxes of new dresses, shoes, and fabric. Marie Antoinette had made so many purchases that the driver had to secure some trunks on top of the carriage with rope. Louise hoped the already shaky stagecoach wouldn't topple over.

There was no money involved in the transaction; the dauphine simply had to sign her name in a thick leather-bound ledger where Rose Bertin tallied up her accounts. *Who, exactly, pays for these outfits?* Louise had wondered. *And what would a shopping spree like this cost?* The young royal reminded her of a high-school girl with unlimited access to her parents' platinum American Express card. She

remembered back to Miss Morris's lesson about historical France's unfair system of taxation where the poorest people wound up paying for the excessive lifestyle of the monarchy. People like Pierre's family. It was so unfair and she was starting to regret the puce gown she had just ordered.

Marie Antoinette looked at her with a raised eyebrow, as though no one had ever asked her why she shopped so much before. "Well, because I can," she eventually replied with a giggle, drawing a childish-looking heart in the foggy window of the carriage with her fingertip. "I'm simply terrified of being bored."

"But you can do other things, too. What about painting or reading or dancing?" Louise definitely needed to get this girl another hobby before she bankrupted the whole country.

"I suppose choosing my clothing is the only decision I'm really allowed to make for myself. I can't decide who I should marry or where I should live or what I shall do, but I am free to decide what I may wear and how I would like to style my hair and what jewels I would like to put around my neck. These are the only freedoms I truly have—to pick the color and fabric of my dress. Is that silly?" she asked, wiping the glass clean with her small palm.

"I guess not," Louise replied quietly. It seemed as though Marie Antoinette's whole life was mapped out for her without her consent and she was just along for the horse-drawn-carriage ride. Louise may not have had nearly as much money as this girl, but at least she had more choices.

"Look at all the women in the court who want to copy me. I've started a fashion revolution. That is power, now, isn't it?"

Louise looked down at her own blush-colored satin dress, no doubt a less magnificent replica of something Marie Antoinette wore the week or the month before. She agreed that, in a way, that *was* power, in the hands of a young woman who was otherwise under the control of her critical mother, her awkward husband, and his father, the king of France. It was similar to being the popular girl in middle school, like when Brooke wore a particular Ella Moss striped top and it felt like the rest of the school had their own versions within a week. Marie Antoinette was definitely the most popular girl in school, or rather, Versailles.

She had clearly started a fashion revolution, but Louise knew if she wasn't careful with her spending and her outward display of riches, Marie Antoinette was going to be starting another sort of revolution as well. A much more violent and bloody one that would mean not only the end of the monarchy, but also the end of the dauphine's and her friends' and family's lives. Maybe Gabrielle's as well. As Louise stared out the cloudy window at the gray passing landscape, her excitement over her first Parisian shopping spree continued turning into more of a gnawing anxiety, and she decided she needed to get her blue Fashionista dress from its secret spot in the armoire, just in case. She didn't want to be trapped in a violent past with no way out.

CHAPTER 26

"What do you think of this one?"

After a several-hours-long journey from Paris, as the horses seemed to be traveling at about the speed that Louise walked because the carriage weight had doubled over the course of their shopping excursion, the girls finally arrived back at the Petit Trianon and were playing dress-up in their new fabulous acquisitions. Or rather, Marie Antoinette was modeling a purple ostrich-feather hat for Adelaide, who had been eagerly waiting at the playhouse for them to return, while Louise was trying to discreetly search the bedroom armoire for her blue dress from the Traveling Fashionista Sale.

Adelaide seemed very curious about what they had purchased, as though she were taking inventory. "Ooh, you got this dress as well?" she asked as she ran her fingers intently along the intricate lace trims, feeling the texture carefully and deliberately as though she were a spy or a fashion student.

"These mother-of-pearl buttons are to die for," she sighed, picking up a pair of long ivory evening gloves. Her attention to detail actually kind of reminded Louise of herself. "I wish you had told me you were going to Paris," Adelaide stated grumpily.

But Louise was presently a tad distracted, as her foolproof hiding spot for the magical dress seemed to be eluding even her. "Madame, do you know where that blue gown is? The one that I was wearing yesterday?" she asked, moving aside some crinoline undergarments. "I could have sworn I left it here in the wardrobe."

"I was so bored of that dress," Marie Antoinette responded with an actual yawn. "You wore it out at least two times in my presence! I do wish you would be more considerate, Gabrielle. I'm very sensitive to those things."

"Okay, I'm sorry about that, but do you know where it is?" Louise dropped any pretense and frantically rummaged through the pink, green, and white dresses on the floor of the armoire. Every color, it seemed, but that distinct robin's egg blue!

"Now, dear Gabrielle, didn't I just buy you another, more beautiful one this morning? No need to be sentimental. I'll personally have Rose Bertin make you another lovely puce frock if you'd like. Something less formal for our garden jaunts."

"I apologize, but with all due respect," Louise began, trying not to lose her composure, as the dauphine could probably have her locked up or even worse for challenging her, "I need my dress back. That one was special. It had sentimental value." Adelaide raised an eyebrow, perhaps surprised that she would dare speak back to Marie Antoinette. Or perhaps because...she had taken it herself? "Wait, do you have it?" Louise turned her attention toward the older woman, who seemed particularly interested in her clothing and whom she had found searching Gabrielle's wardrobe only the day before.

"Why, why would I have it?" Adelaide stammered, blushing and looking away. Louise couldn't help but think she looked guilty! But why would she want her old dresses? Didn't she have her own? Was she jealous of Gabrielle? There was no way they were even the same size.

"My dear Duchesse de Polignac, it is impossible to know where one particular dress is. It is gone. The servants probably gave it away. There are thousands of people living here at Versailles. How am I to know who has it?" Marie Antoinette interjected crossly, clearly getting annoyed. Louise knew it was bad news when her own mother used her full name, so she had a feeling she might be in big trouble if she continued to push this question.

"I hate puce," Louise mumbled sadly to herself. "It looks

like flea puke." It was the only thing Louise could think of to say, feeling overwhelmed that Marie Antoinette wouldn't help her find her dress because she wore it...twice! *Say what?* She was going to be stuck in the eighteenth century because the dauphine was bored?! That dress needed to be found right away.

CHAPTER 27

Adelaide quickly excused herself and rushed out of the play-house after telling the girls about some appointment at the palace she was late for. Or, as Louise was starting to suspect, to hide the stolen dress? Marie Antoinette apparently did not want to be left alone, so despite her annoyance, she asked Louise to stay and play with her and the ever-present pack of little dogs. Louise remembered that when Marie Antoinette asked sweetly for something, it wasn't exactly a question. It was an order. She was used to getting exactly what she wanted.

The dauphine twirled around the room in her new sun-shine yellow frock, fanning herself with a matching silk fan, totally oblivious to Louise's situation, among other things. Like the fact that most of France would later start a huge revolt while she hid in her playhouse trying on more dresses.

"Have some strawberries," she giggled, taking a juicy bite

of a perfectly ripe red berry plucked from a bowl brimming with other perfectly ripe berries. They almost didn't look real. "You used to be so much more fun. What's gotten into you lately, Gabrielle? All that worrying will ruin your complexion."

"No, thank you," Louise replied, sadly closing the heavy walnut door to the armoire. "I find it hard to have fun when so many are suffering." *And when we may be losing our heads literally*, she thought glumly.

"But do you not see that it is always like this? I bet even if you were born hundreds of years from now there would still be human suffering and there would still be parties. I guess I would just prefer to be invited to the party," Marie Antoinette declared, petting her tiny dog, which was playing with a spool of ribbon spilling out of one of the shopping bags.

Louise suddenly felt like a big hypocrite. The dauphine had a point. There was definitely still poverty and suffering in the modern-day world, even though Louise didn't really see any of it firsthand in her hometown. Plus, the reason why she had found the blue dress in the first place was Brooke's fancy-dress party, which she had to admit she was still looking forward to more than anything. If she ever made it back in time.

Louise swore she would be more aware and sensitive in her own life if she got out of here. Her father lost his job and she had to give up her class trip, but her family never had to worry about where the next meal was coming from (even if the next meal happened to be another mushy and tasteless casserole). But there were still girls her age who didn't have a home or a hot meal. She had seen such places and stories on the nightly news and she realized then that in a way she had created her own version of Versailles. She guessed maybe most people did.

"It's simply too awful to think about these things!" Marie Antoinette exclaimed, wiping the red berry stain from her chin with the back of her tiny hand.

"But you must!" Louise urged. She had to get through to her new friend. "You have the power to change things. One day you will be the queen of France...."

"Let's have a macaroon. Isn't the pistachio simply divine?" the young royal interrupted, picking up a pretty pale green cookie and taking a delicate nibble. There was always something delicious only an arm's-length away.

"You can't live in a bubble forever. Believe me on this one." Louise placed her hand on the dauphine's arm. "Those people looked hungry."

"My dear Gabrielle, how would you know what I can and can't do?" Marie Antoinette laughed her gay, airy laugh and dropped the half-eaten pastry carelessly on the white linen tablecloth. "Let them eat cake," she sang under her breath.

"Excuse me?" Louise asked. "What does that even mean?"

If the French people didn't even have bread, how in the world were they supposed to get cake?

"Nothing, silly, I didn't say anything at all," Marie Antoinette replied with a shrug, as though the whole thing were a figment of her royal companion's overactive imagination. With that, she picked up her shih tzu and pranced out the glass French doors to frolic in the garden as if she didn't have a care in the world.

CHAPTER 28

Louise dashed out of the house, through the playhouse gates, and back through the geometric gardens toward Versailles. A dark rain cloud passed over the late afternoon sun, giving the vast grounds a dark and creepy aura. She had a feeling things were changing and not just the weather. She wanted to find Pierre. He was the only one who might believe her and help her get back home. Somehow. He just had to help her find the blue dress.

"*Excusez-moi*, have you seen Pierre?" she asked an old wrinkled groundsman who was tilling soil in a freshly made flower bed.

"I know no Pierre," he responded quietly without looking up. She asked another woman, who was gathering up roses in her apron. "Pierre? I do not believe there is any Pierre working in these gardens."

Had she completely made this guy up in her imagination?

Was he a spy or was he fired because they were seen together? Nothing was making any sense, and the overcast sky was starting to drizzle....

"Pierre no longer works at Versailles," a voice behind her announced in a low, gravelly baritone.

Louise spun around to see what must have been the head gardener, a pock-faced man with a mean scowl, looking at her with his arms crossed defensively across his chest. "He was relieved of his duties this morning. For distributing propaganda against the dauphine. May I help you with something?"

"No, I'm fine," Louise stammered, her eyes getting watery to hear of Pierre's upsetting dismissal and with the sudden realization that the only person who would even possibly believe her was gone. She lowered her head before the sour-looking gardener could see her cry and took off running toward the palace.

In her haste, she took an unfamiliar turn and the garden turned into a complicated labyrinth with its towering shrubs, making Louise feel like she was a fancily dressed rat trapped in a maze. As she turned and continued walking faster and deeper into the lush green maze, the panic started to well up in her throat and her left temple started throbbing as though she were on the verge of a migraine. What if she never found her way home? She had wanted to escape her life so badly once again, but from this perspective, nothing in Fairview, Connecticut, seemed so awful anymore.

Louise paused and tried to take a deep breath, but the whalebone corset underneath her structured blush-colored dress made it almost impossible for her to get any oxygen. She started to feel faint, so she leaned against the ten-foot-high hedges to get her balance. Dark, menacing clouds continued to roll in and a low roar of thunder echoed in the distance. A storm was definitely coming.

She glimpsed two dark, shadowy figures in wide-brimmed, feathered hats ahead of her. Maybe they could get her out of this interminable maze? She turned another corner, but they were just a few steps too quick and darted out of reach, alluding her grasp.

"Please stop. Maybe you can help me!" Louise called out to them, but the rumbling storm cloud was now directly overhead, drowning out her words. The elusive silhouettes didn't turn around; it was as if she wasn't even there. She ran after them, tripping over her long cumbersome skirts, then turned another tall, hedged corner and was spit out into the grand front lawn of Versailles, totally alone and damp under the cloudy gray sky.

CHAPTER 29

Louise gathered her hooped skirts and raced back up the white marble stone steps of the enormous palace, coming to a skidding stop when she realized that she had walked directly into a long, intimidating hall lined with mirrors.

The grandeur of the space was overwhelming. The massive room was aglow with three rows of silver chandeliers running down the wide hall, the white candlelight bouncing off the square panes of mirror and glass. Louise counted seventeen mirrored arcades opposite seventeen tall arched windows overlooking the gardens. Bronze cherub statues held up crystal candelabras like illuminated offerings. Maroon-and-white marble columns leading up to a ceiling painted with dark oily reds and blues of various battle scenes gave off the impression that whoever lived in this palace was powerful and very rich.

For someone in Louise's particular condition, the Hall of

Mirrors was a trap, a place where it would be almost impossible to hide who she really was. After the menacing Dr. Hastings was able to see her true identity in the glass reflection on the *Titanic*, and as Louise most recently did again in the gilded mirror at Petit Trianon, there was a very real possibility she would be discovered. And unfortunately for her, the Hall of Mirrors was also the main artery that ran through Versailles. She would have to take a major detour back out through the garden terrace to avoid it, and it was now raining hard. Louise didn't know what her hair did when it rained in eighteenth-century France, but she was all too familiar with the frizzy mess of the twenty-first century.

Out of a combination of vanity and haste, she decided to risk it. Miraculously, at this moment the hall was completely deserted. She would walk as fast as possible with her head down, praying that no one noticed the million Louise Lamberts being reflected in the huge arched mirrors that lined the seemingly endless hallway. She cautiously stepped into the long, empty room and her mouth shaped into a surprised *O* to once again see her real reflection, at age twelve, looking back at her from beyond the glass, her familiar hazel eyes peeking out from underneath Gabrielle's sky-high pouf. She took a moment to twirl around and admire her satin hoopskirt couture ball gown. As she smiled at her spinning image, the shiny flash of her braces ricocheted off the polished, mirrored reflections down the hall like a silver echo. Louise quickly closed her mouth, lowered her head toward the ground, and took off running down the freshly waxed corridor.

She hadn't made it more than halfway down the otherwise deserted grand promenade when out of the corner of her eye she noticed the Princesse de Lamballe and Adelaide heading directly toward her. They couldn't see her like this! She stopped running and kept her head down as they crossed paths, desperately hoping they would fail to recognize one of their closest companions.

"Good afternoon, my dear Gabrielle," the Princesse de Lamballe sang.

Louise did a slight curtsey and, against her better judgment, was compelled to look up. The Princesse de Lamballe continued walking, playfully chasing a small dog with huge floppy ears down the hallway, but Louise's number-one dress-stealing suspect, Adelaide, had stopped frozen and was staring at her with her mouth agape. Louise had been discovered!

She tried not to look in the mirror the way you try not to look at a car accident on the side of the highway when you know it's going to be awful but something inside you compels you to do it anyway. What she saw almost made her scream.

It wasn't the face of Adelaide.

It was the reflection of another twelve-ish-year-old girl

with a mouthful of silver braces with pink elastics, staring openmouthed and wide-eyed at Louise.

Ohmigod!

Louise's jaw dropped toward the freshly polished parquet floor.

After a moment of complete and utter shock, the girl quickly looked away and ran out of the Hall of Mirrors, awkwardly clattering across the tiles in her old-fashioned high-heeled slippers.

Louise slipped out of her yellow diamond-buckled heels and took off after her, no longer caring if she caused a scene. She needed to catch this girl and find out exactly what was going on!

"Gabrielle? Adelaide?" the Princesse de Lamballe called out after them in her sweet, concerned voice. "What in heavens has gotten into you two?"

Louise didn't slow down to answer. If what she had just seen wasn't a crazy hallucination brought on by too many sugary macaroons, then she had just come across another Traveling Fashionista. In eighteenth-century France. *Say what?*

CHAPTER 30

The woman was waiting for her at the other end of the hall-way. She was hiding behind the tall salon door and popped out when Louise ran by.

"Quick, who is your favorite designer?" she asked in a loud whisper.

"Right now it's Yves Saint Laurent," a completely startled Louise answered without thinking. "Oops, I mean…" She paused, her mind racing. Why was Adelaide asking her this? Dead silence.

"No waaay! You're a part of the club." Louise looked at the older woman. On the outside, it was still exactly as if she were having a conversation with Adelaide. But she wasn't.

"What did you just say?" Louise asked, taken aback.

"You're a Traveling Fashionista. I knew something was different about you. But I can't believe Marla and Glenda allowed for us to cross paths in the past. That's against the rules."

Marla and Glenda? This woman knew Marla and Glenda? "How do you know about them?" Louise replied, aghast.

"Because I'm a Traveling Fashionista, too!" the woman exclaimed as though this was the most obvious thing in the world. "But I can't believe this would be allowed to happen," she continued, throwing her hands up at the craziness of it all.

"Well... well, they didn't exactly let me take this trip," Louise stammered, realizing that she could be in big trouble the next time she saw the two unsuspecting and easily angered shopkeepers. "Technically, I tried on the dress when they weren't looking."

Adelaide, or whoever the girl was, gave Louise a stern look. "Like I said, that's against the rules."

"What rules?" This whole conversation was totally blowing Louise's mind. She didn't care if she was making a scene, because she had a gazillion questions to ask.

"Shhh," the girl whispered crossly. "They can't be allowed to hear us. *No one* but us can know about this. But come on now, clearing the dirty dishes from the table, flirting with the gardener, confusing me for the Princesse de Lamballe. I'd say you were being rather obvious about the whole thing."

"How am I supposed to act? I'm not even sure where or who I am," Louise replied defensively. "Is that girl actually *the* Marie Antoinette? And who are you, anyway?"

"Of course that's Marie Antoinette! My name is Stella. But here you should obviously call me Adelaide."

"How old are you really?" Louise asked.

"Thirteen. I'm from Manhattan. You?"

"Twelve. I'm from Fairview, Connecticut. But my dad used to work in the city. . . ." Louise responded quickly, eager to get the small talk out of the way so she could focus on the important things, like getting back to the twenty-first century.

"So in suburban years I'm, like, sixteen," Stella continued, cutting Louise off midthought.

"I didn't realize there was a difference." Were suburban years like dog years?

"Clearly." Stella nodded, cocking an eyebrow.

This girl might like vintage, but she wasn't being very cool.

"How did you become a Traveling Fashionista?" Louise asked. Had Stella received a mysterious invitation to the Fashionista Sale, too?

"Fashion is in my blood!" Stella exclaimed proudly. "My great-great-aunt twice removed was Coco Chanel."

"That's awesome," Louise squealed. She wanted to feign indifference, but she was actually totally impressed. This girl was twice removed from fashion royalty! Coco Chanel was arguably the most influential designer of the twentieth century.

"The incredible power of vintage—the fact that energy

can't be destroyed, that by wearing vintage we are wearing the past and other women's histories on our bodies and bringing them into the present, even the future. I just get it," Stella declared in a tone that implied that despite all evidence to the contrary, Louise did not. "Isn't it in your family, too?"

"I don't think so." Louise shook her head, thinking of how against anything "used" her mother was. Her father probably didn't know what the word *vintage* even meant, but then again there was her glamorous actress great-aunt Alice Baxter whom she discovered on board the *Titanic* and who had loved beautiful dresses. Perhaps it was in her blood after all? "Well, maybe; I'm not quite sure. How many of us are there?"

"Maybe five? Ten?" Stella answered hesitantly. Louise was having a hard time reconciling this older woman's face with the girl she had seen in the Hall of Mirrors. "Actually, I don't really know. You're the first one I've met. I kind of thought it was just me."

"Me too," Louise agreed. "Is this really happening?" She pinched herself hard on her arm.

"I don't know, but it feels real, doesn't it?"

"Yeah. So maybe it doesn't matter."

"Aren't these clothes to die for?" Stella whispered to her, pointing to a woman passing by who was wearing an elaborate salmon-colored gown whose silk was embroidered with a blue-and-green vine pattern. On top of her pouf, she wore a

flat hat that had a bouquet of actual blue-and-green flowers somehow stuck into it. "It kills me that they don't make anything like them anymore. The detail that goes into each button, each piece of trim. You can see its influence everywhere hundreds of years later. The House of Dior designed an entire collection based on this moment in history." In that instant Louise got a glimpse of the modern thirteen-year-old fashion geek inside the uppity old-fashioned packaging.

"But these corsets are torture," Louise whispered loudly, putting her hands on her hips. "I've almost fainted, like, three times so far."

"Right?" Stella snorted and laughed a lot like Brooke did, inadvertently chipping away her ice-queen image and giving Louise another peek at the teenage girl she truly was. Maybe they could be friends after all?

"Walk with me." Stella linked her arm through Louise's, and they continued strolling through the adjacent salon. "So tell me, how do I look?" she asked excitedly. "I can't see myself. Every time I see a mirror, it's me. I've discovered that Adelaide is the daughter of Louis's father, King Louis XV of France!"

"Ummm..." Louise gulped. How was she going to tell her new comrade she looked like an old stout woman with a permanent scowl?

"I think Adelaide is such a fabulous name. Maybe I'll switch permanently."

"Honestly?"

"Of course!"

"Well," Louise started, trying to phrase things in the most delicate way possible. "You're, how do I say, advanced in your years...."

"Old? I'm old??" Stella stopped walking and turned toward Louise, now giving her her full attention.

"That's another word for it."

"Do I have wrinkles?"

"I'm not sure." Louise shrugged diplomatically.

"You're not sure? Are you looking at me or what?"

"I guess you're kind of, um, unattractive? But it's okay, Stella. I'm sure in real life you're very pretty!"

"I'm old and ugly? Argh! Why did Marla and Glenda do this to me? Is this a kooky joke?"

"And, um," Louise started, taking in a whiff of stale body odor, "you kind of smell."

"What?!" Stella grabbed Louise's arms tightly, her fingernails digging into her skin. "This is *soo* embarrassing."

"It's not really you," Louise tried to assure her. "Besides, from what I've experienced, everyone smells in this era."

"But you're young and beautiful. It's not fair!"

"It's not me," Louise protested, running her hand along the seam of her full silk skirt. "It's Gabrielle and the dress."

"But still. Look, my dress is more beautiful," Stella

gestured to her elaborate spearmint-colored court gown. "And everyone is so respectful of me."

"Right. Look on the bright side. You have a higher rank than me. Apparently you're the daughter of the king. I guess you can't judge a lady by her gown."

"What do you mean by that?"

"Maybe Marla and Glenda are trying to teach us a lesson. Like I apparently need more self-confidence, and maybe you're learning about how looks don't mean everything?"

"Well, I want my old life back. I'm out of here. I hate the name Adelaide," Stella decided, furiously pacing back and forth.

"You can't leave me!" Louise cried urgently, grabbing Adelaide's gloved hand. "I think my blue dress was stolen. I need your help."

"I'll tell you everything you need to know tonight, but then I must get back," she said under her breath just as the Princesse de Lamballe caught up with them in the salon and struck a confused look.

"Is anything the matter?" the perplexed blonde girl asked them.

"Of course not. Everything is fine. Until tonight, Gabrielle," Stella responded quickly. With that, she snapped back into character and Adelaide gave Louise a slight curtsey, then glided out of the room with the princess as though this were just an ordinary afternoon at Versailles.

CHAPTER 31

Louise made her way back into Gabrielle's suite and leaned against the heavy gilded door with a sigh. She needed a minute to herself to absorb everything. It took only a moment before she realized that she wasn't alone. "How did you get here?" she asked, startled.

Glenda was draped over the king-size platform bed wearing a deep purple velvet cloak lined with bloodred silk. She was teasing a fluffy gray kitten with a long green-and-blue peacock feather. Marla had squeezed into a midnight black floor-length corseted gown, accented with glimmering ruby buttons running down the bodice that seemed as if they were about to pop if she made any sudden movements. She was eagerly helping herself to some glossy grapes left on a silver platter on the gold leaf side table.

"What kind of a welcome is that?" Glenda's eyes sparkled at Louise.

"Aren't you happy to see us?" Marla asked sadly. "It was a bit of a journey, you know," she added, fingering the antique-looking poodle necklace she seemed to always wear around her neck.

"Believe me, am I ever happy to see you!" Louise gushed. "Please, how do I make the dauphine understand the seriousness of the situation going on outside the palace gates? Maybe we can help stop the revolution if we can only get her to see the poverty and suffering happening right in front of her eyes."

"Sometimes it's hardest to see what is right in front of you," Marla replied cryptically.

"So how can I show her?" Louise asked in a trembling voice. "If we don't do something, the French people will starve and the whole royal family will be killed!"

"Meddling with history!" Glenda exclaimed as the kitten she was tickling let out a loud meow. "A rather dangerous preoccupation."

"Try not to be so morbid, my dear. Ooh, your dress is fabulous. Glenda, we do need some new inventory...." Marla changed the subject, fingering the satin of Louise's dress. "And as you should know from previous experiences, there's only so much one can affect what has already passed."

"Why didn't you tell me about Stella and the other Fashionistas?" Louise suddenly blurted out, hands on her hips.

"She wants everything to be spelled out, now, doesn't she? What fun is there in that?" Glenda asked in her deep husky voice that sent the startled kitten scurrying off the gold-embroidered coverlet.

"We thought we had given you quite a bit of information to work with in your letter. Of course you should discover some things on your own. That's how you grow." Marla popped a purple orb into her mouth. "They don't make 'em like they used to," she added, mopping the juice off her several stray chin hairs with her dress sleeve.

"Exactly how many Fashionistas are there? When can I meet them?" Louise asked eagerly, and then plopped down on a nearby chaise. This was all getting to be too much for her. Why did she feel like she was always working with about two percent of the pertinent information?

"All in due course. Although this is not exactly the way we would have planned it," Glenda said, standing up from the bed in one quick intimidating movement. At her full height, she towered over Marla and Louise like they were toddlers playing dress-up.

"I'm sorry," Louise apologized. "I should have asked to try the dress on. I just had a feeling it was meant for me. Like I was destined to go on this journey."

"Well, sweet pea, it's nice to feel special for a bit and to feel as though you are the chosen one. As we can see by the way you left poor Brooke. She's supposed to be your best friend," Marla reminded her gently. The thought of the way she had treated Brooke almost made Louise cry.

"That girl has made some remarkable changes. Once we got her out of that horrendous tracksuit and into more suitable attire, we were almost ready to make her an honorary member," Glenda declared, holding up one of Gabrielle's fabulous sapphire-and-diamond bracelets from the ebony jewelry box on the vanity table.

"I miss Brooke. I want to go back to my real life."

"You are part of a very select group now. Not just anyone can be chosen," Marla continued, blatantly avoiding Louise's request.

"Maybe we'll throw a fabulous party for all our Fashionistas once you make it back. Then you gals can chat. Haven't you always wanted to be part of a group of girls who know the difference between a Versace and a Givenchy? Who can lend you a Pucci minidress for your next exciting event? They're the only ones in the world who can possibly know what you're going through." That was exactly what Louise wanted, but she wasn't sure how Brooke fit into this equation. If she ever got back to Fairview, things would be different. She didn't want to grow apart from her best friend, but maybe there was no way to stop it. It hurt to think about it.

"Of course that does mean you'll have to make it back

first," Marla reminded her in a hushed tone. Not like she needed any reminding. "And France does seem to be on the eve of a revolution."

"Our hands are tied, my dear. This time you truly did get yourself into a pickle," Glenda declared as she let the jeweled bangle fall to the glass tabletop with a harsh and startling clatter.

"Quite sneaky. We turned our backs for one moment and—poof!" Marla snapped her fingers.

"Well, she *is* almost a teenager, Marla. They're known to sneak out of the house sometimes."

"And Marie Antoinette is probably not the best influence," Marla decided with a disapproving *tsk*.

"But you're a resourceful girl. If you were able to find your way here without our assistance, we're sure you'll be able to find your way back. Hopefully with a new understanding about your current situation," Glenda remarked ominously.

"The past can teach you a lot, my dear. Now I'm starting to sound like a broken Victrola." Just as Marla swallowed another grape, the top ruby button on her bodice shot across the room like a jeweled missile. "Oops!" she exclaimed, her cheeks turning as crimson as her missing button.

"Perhaps your modern problems, like your father losing his job, aren't so modern after all. Financial crisis? Do you think there wasn't a financial crisis in pre-revolutionary France?

These days you can't even walk the streets of Paris without someone trying to pluck the rubies right off your bodice," Glenda said, throwing Marla a pointed look.

"I suppose I've gained a kilo or two since the last time I wore this one." Marla shook her head.

"Now, I would say your problems have gotten a bit more serious than missing a trip to Europe," Glenda added, drawing an ominous line across her throat with a long red fingernail. The universal sign for major problems and, in this case, literally losing her head—which had just taken on a whole new terrifying and real meaning.

Suddenly there was a sharp rap on the bedroom door.

"Can you guys, like, hide or something?" Louise asked, panicked, lifting up the heavy red satin bedskirt.

"Already embarrassed of us?" Glenda muttered under her breath. "Kids these days…"

As Louise turned to open the door while smoothing her dress and trying futilely to compose herself, she smelled a strong waft of musky French perfume and spun around to see that her intergalactic tour guides had vanished into a royal purple cloud of violet-scented mist. She shook her head, bewildered by their dramatic exit.

Gabrielle's two personal maids, Miss String Bean and Miss Stout, as Louise now referred to them in her head, marched in carrying a gorgeous carnation pink ball gown

with light pink ruffled trim before she even had a chance to reach for the doorknob. Why they bothered knocking at all was a mystery to her.

"Time to prepare for supper," Miss String Bean announced with her hands clasped together. For once Louise had lost her appetite. All she could think about was finding Stella and getting back to the twenty-first century before it was too late.

With an awkward curtsey, Miss Stout handed Louise a folded slip of ivory stationery that was tucked into the folds of her ginormous bosom.

Dearest Gabrielle,
Please meet me by the reflecting pools after dusk.
We have much to discuss.

It wasn't signed, but that note could only have come from one person. It seemed as though Stella had found her instead. Louise smiled and placed the note on a nearby end table. That was exactly the message she was hoping she'd receive.

CHAPTER 32

Dinner that night was held in a grand formal dining room in an entirely new wing of the palace with one long table set up in the center of the large, ornately decorated space. Dusk couldn't come fast enough—when Louise really wanted to talk to Stella. Her conversation with Marla and Glenda had been unbelievably frustrating. Why couldn't they just speak plainly to her instead of making puzzle pieces out of her fate?

She anxiously picked at the gelatinous food that had been set before her by an army of uniformed waiters. There must have been at least a thousand people working at Versailles at any given time. The evening meal was chopped-up pieces of meat and vegetables suspended in a bell-shaped, amber-colored Jell-O mold. Even her mother wouldn't make something this unappealing, she thought as she tapped the quivering form with her spoon. With all the delicious pastries she had consumed so far, she was a little surprised to see dinner was so gross.

She was seated next to the Princesse de Lamballe, the only person in the room whom Louise recognized. The princess was sweetly making small talk with the guests around them as she delicately ate her mystery meat. Marie Antoinette had a headache, the princess explained, and was taking supper in her private chamber. Adelaide was also noticeably absent from the long dining table, and every time a new guest entered the dining hall, Louise would whip her head around in nervous anticipation. But the woman who she now knew was Stella never arrived. Where was she?

Soon the table was cleared, the grating harpsichord music was starting, and the ever-present platters of sweets were being paraded out of the wings by unsmiling uniformed waiters.

It didn't take much time before Louise could no longer concentrate on all of the excess and sweets and fashion. Okay, maybe not the fashion part. That aspect was still pretty awesome. Now, mostly all she could think about was that she had to meet Stella wherever she was. She was ready to go home.

"*Excusez-moi*, may I have this dance?" a mustached man in an embroidered tailcoat asked, tapping the Princesse de Lamballe on her shoulder.

"*Oui*," she replied with a blush, accepting his outstretched hand and letting him lead her out to the now crowded dance floor.

Louise quickly seized this opportunity to sneak out of the

party, as there seemed to be a party every night in Versailles, and walked out to the terrace. It was dusk and the reflecting pools cast a beautiful moonlit shadow over the palace.

Then she realized she wasn't alone. A black gloved hand grabbed her upper arm in a surprisingly strong grip.

"Follow me," a voice whispered behind her.

Startled, Louise spun around to see a pale, shadowy female face hidden inside a dark velvet-hooded cloak. Before she could get a good look at her, the figure turned and began walking quickly down the dark garden path.

"Umm, Stella, this is a little creepy. Can't we just, like, talk here, where there's candlelight?"

The cloaked figure motioned for Louise to follow her.

"Whatever you want," Louise sighed, trying not to let her nerves get the better of her as she hesitantly followed her guide into the darkness.

They eventually arrived in the middle of a clearing, and the girl stopped abruptly, lowering her hood. But it wasn't Stella!

"I'm glad you received my note. I wanted you to know that I had to send Adelaide on an official expedition to Vienna. I think she was spying on me," Marie Antoinette stated calmly, holding the dark velvet hood at her shoulders.

"You did what?!" Louise asked in total shock, realizing the one link to her real life had just been banished from Versailles. "But—but why?"

"She had been acting so peculiar lately. Like a complete stranger! Asking detailed questions about every piece of clothing I purchased. I think she was sending reports back to my mother. The details my mother wrote in her letters proved to me that she has the ear of someone close to me. I've never trusted Adelaide, and I need to be sure I can trust everyone in my inner circle. Can I trust you, Gabrielle? You are now my dearest friend...aren't you?" The question hovered in the chilly night air, almost like a threat.

"Of course," Louise stuttered. Her mind was racing. Stella must have known where her blue dress was, and now she was gone! "But I need to find Adelaide. I'm quite sure this is a huge mistake."

"It's futile," Marie Antoinette said with an indifferent shrug. "She should be almost at the border by this hour."

"I'm sorry, please excuse me, I...I need to go now."

Louise ran back up the vast lawn toward the palace. She needed to find Stella and had no idea where to even begin now! What if they were now both trapped in the past forever? She skidded to a stop and asked one of the staunch entryway guards if he had seen Madame Adelaide leave in a carriage. He said nothing and just looked down at her with a quiet, stony stare.

Louise kept running and burst open the third door on the

left, where Stella's, or rather Adelaide's, bedroom was. Two chambermaids were silently stripping the bedsheets.

"Is Adelaide here?" she asked breathlessly.

"No, mademoiselle, she had to travel to Austria immediately. It was a diplomatic matter for the state."

Louise was too late.

"When did she leave?" Louise asked frantically.

"Before supper. But she left you this note."

The maid handed her a sealed letter that had been propped up on the bedside table, addressed to Duchesse de Polignac in a fancy script. She immediately ripped it open with trembling fingers.

Louise,

The note began in a sloppy, teenage penmanship, much different from the flawless calligraphy on the cream-colored envelope. This had clearly been written in a hurry. A dark ink blot was splotched on the lower corner.

I will see you on the other side. Be careful, we are all under suspicion! The dauphine does not trust anyone. The revolution must go on. It is time to set back the clocks before it's too late.

But how could Louise get back to the other side without her dress? Why hadn't Stella left her the blue gown instead of a cryptic note? Louise put her head in her hands as she sat at the foot of the massive bed. And what did she mean by setting back the clocks? Clocks had nothing to do with anything! Her eyes wandered around the room and fell on a golden clock in a bell jar on the fireplace mantel across the room. Or was this some sort of clue? She ran over to the fireplace and carefully picked up the clock, hoping to find another note underneath. Nothing. Louise slowly lowered herself to the ground in her big pink hoop skirt, feeling utterly defeated.

Then she saw the faint glimmer of robin's egg blue peeking out of the fireplace hearth. She frantically pushed aside the screen and saw her lost dress rolled up into a messy satin and lace ball. She could have kissed it! Stella had come through for her! One Traveling Fashionista looking out for the other.

Holding the magical blue gown in her hand, Louise was suddenly unsure of what to do. Had she accomplished anything at all on this trip? She didn't think she'd been able to wake Marie Antoinette up to the harsh reality of her own people. Yet she knew the longer she stayed, the riskier it became. Maybe Stella was right that the revolution was inevitable and necessary, that the French people needed a change.

Louise heard the yipping of a dog skittering down the

cavernous marble hallway. A moment later, Macaroon nudged the bedroom door open with his fluffy white head and ran over to her, jumping up on the gown in Louise's hands and nipping at the silk fabric.

"Down," she laughed, trying to pull the dress away from the puppy's tiny but surprisingly strong jaw. Macaroon pulled harder, and Louise found herself in a tug-of-war with the overindulged shih tzu. "Let go," Louise whispered as nicely as she could through clenched teeth. The dog growled back at her.

"Macaroon!" a familiar high-pitched voice called from the hall. "Where are you, my precious?"

The small white fluffy dog cocked his ear, paused, and looked toward the door, giving Louise the moment she needed to yank the blue dress free. Now she was really ready to leave.

"Macaroon!" The dauphine's voice got closer, and the dog yipped excitedly, running across the room. Louise yanked off her present outfit, ripping the delicate carnation-pink fabric in her haste, and hopped into the cumbersome blue hoopskirt without a second to lose. She had just barely pulled up the fitted bodice when the gold doorknob turned and Marie Antoinette stepped into the suite, still dressed in her dark floor-length velvet cloak.

"Hello, my little..."

Louise looked directly into the dauphine's surprised blue

eyes before she felt as if the parquet floor split open below her, and she was instantly sucked down, falling and falling fast through a pile of petticoats.

A barrage of images flashed in front of Louise as she fell, like stop-motion frames from a 3-D movie. Marie Antoinette sweating and weak in her bed and being handed a screaming infant while surrounded by a claustrophobic crowd of people; an angry mob of women marching in front of Versailles with meat cleavers; an older-looking Marie Antoinette terrified and escaping through a secret doorway by her bed; the distraught queen of France gaunt and exhausted, wearing a simple sack dress, sitting alone on a thin mattress in a prison cell; the beautiful face of the Princesse de Lamballe separated from her body and floating in space; a barely recognizable Marie Antoinette looking like a frail old woman dressed in a thin white nightdress, tripping as she is led up the wooden steps to her certain death. Finally, Louise saw the grand palace of Versailles aflame, fire shooting out of enormous broken windows, the marble façade crumbling down to the ground in a pile of dust and fiery stone.

Louise thought she might die of a broken heart before she woke up. As the rushing sound of a guillotine swooshed around her, Louise felt the wind as it sliced down. Before she could scream, she opened her eyes.

"There is nothing
new except what has
been forgotten."

MARIE ANTOINETTE,
queen of France,
1774–1792

CHAPTER 33

Louise awoke, heart pounding, lying facedown in a patch of crinoline. She let out a little sneeze as the scratchy fabric tickled her nose, and she heard the low murmur of familiar voices. What happened to her? How long had she been lying here?

Her head was pounding as she wiped a wet streak from her left cheek. Had she been crying in her sleep? She was sprawled out on a low Victorian chaise lounge, her hip bone digging into an uncomfortable hooped structure. She looked down and discovered she was swimming in the antique pale blue dress, a little faded and worn, and a flood of memories from what she'd just experienced washed over her.

"Umm, hello?" she called out hesitantly. Her voice sounded weak but normal. She was definitely speaking English instead of French, and she was pretty sure she was her old self again.

"Where is that other shoe?!" she heard in response. "I know

it's up the chimney somewhere! These would look fabulous on her!"

Louise shakily propped herself up and tried to get her bearings. It appeared she was back inside the stone cottage, once again surrounded by rolling racks of vintage dresses and fur coats and leaning towers of striped hatboxes. "I'm over here!" she called out. Did they forget she existed or something? The two salesladies appeared as soon as the thought crossed her mind.

"Our Fashionista has finally awoken!" Glenda exclaimed, looking down at her with a wink. She was holding out a pair of ruby red Ferragamo wedges for her to try on. "We thought these would be perfect for you. Of course, not with that blue dress." Glenda shook her head disapprovingly at Louise's eighteenth-century French couture gown. "Now that would be a fashion faux pas."

"Why don't you put this back on for now?" Marla offered, handing Louise her familiar navy cardigan sweater and pink-and-white floral Betsey Johnson dress that was covered in grass stains from her spill on the front lawn earlier. There were no hoop skirts or gut-wrenching corsets, and at that moment Louise realized for sure that she was back where she belonged, in the twenty-first century.

"What happened to me?" she asked, shaking her head in disbelief at the crazy adventure she had just been on. Louise smiled as she clutched her favorite Anthropologie sweater tightly to her chest like a teddy bear, so relieved and happy to be back in her real life.

"It looks like you took a little tumble on your bicycle before you came into the shop. An old-fashioned bump on the head."

"You'll be good as new in no time," Marla declared reassuringly.

"Food poisoning, concussions…" Brooke teased as she dropped herself on the Victorian sofa on top of the billowing blue satin skirts. Louise had almost forgotten her friend was at the sale, too. "I think this vintage habit of yours is getting a bit dangerous," she said, giggling.

"Nonsense!" Glenda exclaimed defensively.

"I'm sorry." Louise took Brooke's hand. "I should have told you I was coming to the Traveling Fashionista Sale. We always go shopping together and I broke our pact." Louise looked down, feeling like she might almost cry. She hadn't even realized how upset this had made her until she said it out loud.

"Don't worry," Brooke replied. "And besides, I think I'm starting to learn a bit about vintage style, too." She gave her friend a reassuring hug and held out her hand with a giant yellow cocktail ring sparkling on her finger. "What do you think? Is it too much?"

Louise had a flashback to Marie Antoinette with her giant powdery pouf and had to lie down again. She guessed these were called Victorian fainting couches for a reason. "No, it's perfect. I've just never seen anything quite like it before," she answered, getting a major case of déjà vu. Her head was strangely itchy and she gasped as she pulled out a tiny jeweled hairpin from her tousled frizzy bun. This miniature sparkly diamond was definitely not hers. It was something Gabrielle would wear.

"You just missed this awesome girl who was here. You guys would have *a lot* in common," Brooke continued, carelessly taking off the dazzling ring and tossing it on the sofa. "She's almost as obsessed with vintage as you are. You guys would probably be, like, good friends," she remarked, almost a little sadly.

"Yes, I am sure you and Stella would have a lot to discuss," Marla said, shooting Louise a pointed look as she gathered some discarded clothing from the rough wide-plank hardwood floor. Louise thought she caught a glimpse of Adelaide's long-sleeved beige dress peeking out of the huge ball of clothes Marla had scooped up in her arms.

Wait, Stella was here—and I missed her?!

She looked over at her friend happily texting on her cell phone and realized that Brooke was perfectly content in her own real life. She didn't carry with her the feeling inside that something was missing, as Louise did. That longing for another life, another time, another story. They would always be different in that way.

232

"How do I get in touch with her? Do you have her e-mail address? Or her last name? Is she on Facebook?" Louise needed to meet Stella again. She was the only other person who had any idea what she was going through. She wanted more answers.

"What on earth is a Facebook?" Glenda questioned with a puzzled look. "And do we look like the kind of people who use an e-mail address?" She gestured to a frazzled Marla, who had given up on trying to fold the clothes she was carrying and was now forcefully shoving them behind a potted bamboo plant.

"I guess we should be going, too!" Louise exclaimed once she had changed back into her much more comfortable and familiar floral sundress, navy cardigan, and beloved pink Converse. Apparently Louise was going to have to investigate the true identity of her fellow time-traveling Fashionista on her own. Luckily, her Internet stalking skills were pretty impressive. She would find Stella somehow.

"Let me get a bag for you," Glenda offered, grabbing the delicate blue dress out of Louise's arms and expertly wrapping it up in a large bindle, which she hung on a bamboo stick that she plucked from the plant in the corner. "Hobo chic," she declared happily. "Our new look!"

"You mean I can have this?" Louise asked, almost afraid to take it. "Isn't the dress extremely valuable?"

"We know you'll take marvelous care of it. It could not have a better home or closet," Glenda said with a proud smile.

"Thank you," Louise replied, feeling unbelievably lucky to be back in her old life and with an amazing antique dress to add to her vintage collection.

"A little treat before you go?" Marla displayed a platter of homemade cookies seemingly out of thin air—or perhaps an open hatbox—for them to choose from.

"I think I've had enough sweets for a while." Louise thought back to the stomach-turning excess she had just experienced at Versailles as Brooke happily grabbed a misshapen chocolate chip cookie from the tray. "All the sugar I've been eating lately seems to be giving me a major headache."

She could have sworn she heard the two ladies chuckle quietly together. "Well, we do hope you enjoyed your visit! Please see us again sometime soon, as you know we are constantly discovering fabulous new inventory and accessories. And say hello to your darling mother for us!"

"Don't worry, I'll be back. I mean, we will." Louise smiled at Brooke, no longer feeling the dull pounding in her head. She was so utterly happy and content to be back in Fairview with her best friend. The two girls skipped outside, down the cottage steps, and into the fresh spring afternoon air. Louise hopped on her scuffed but luckily still functioning bicycle, which was splayed out on the front grass next to Brooke's shiny ten-speed, and they headed home with the train of her blue dress blowing in the breeze behind them.

CHAPTER 34

It turned out that Louise did, in fact, have a very mild concussion. Mrs. Lambert took one look at the red bump on her daughter's left temple and immediately called Dr. Jacobs to make a house call. The pediatrician arrived and, judging by his turquoise polo shirt and madras plaid pants, had been called in during a round of Saturday golf. He ordered Louise to spend the remainder of the afternoon in bed and Mrs. Lambert to check on her every few hours. After the day she'd just had, she wasn't going to argue. Besides, this gave her time to research what exactly she had just seen firsthand. She opened her laptop and tented it under her grandmother's patchwork quilt so that her mother wouldn't walk in and bust her when she was supposed to be resting. Louise needed to find out everything she could about Marie Antoinette and the French Revolution.

At fourteen years old, Marie Antoinette was taken by a royal carriage from her childhood home in Austria to France, where she was arranged to marry Louis XVI. Once the horse-drawn carriage came to the midway point of the journey, a bridge over the Rhine River, which was considered neutral territory, she was taken out and led into a small luxuriously decorated set of rooms, where she was completely stripped of her Austrian dress and all her accessories, and even her childhood dog, Mops, was taken from her. She was then given a new French gown and stockings and jewels, as she was from here on out to pledge loyalty to her new country, and any Austrian artifacts she possessed would be seen as treachery.

The hairs on Louise's arms stood up. This scene reminded her of the creepy dream she had the other night before her time-traveling adventure, in which the group of women in the woods dressed her up in the beautiful blue gown and destroyed her old clothes. It was as if she had experienced Marie Antoinette's scary and uncertain journey from her childhood in Austria to her future life in France. She kept reading.

On May 16, 1770, Marie Antoinette and Louis XVI were married in an elaborate ceremony at the chapel of Versailles, officially making her the dauphine of France. Four years after their wedding, King Louis XV unexpectedly died of smallpox, making Louis XVI the reigning king, and therefore, Marie Antoinette, at the young age of nineteen, became the queen of France and Navarre. At the beginning of their reign, the French people fell in love with her beauty, elegance, style, and youth, but before long, the tide of public opinion changed dramatically. Soon, her extravagant lifestyle and copious consumption were mocked, and she was rumored to be an Austrian spy and traitor.

Marie Antoinette also had to deal with her overbearing and cruel mother, who was frequently writing her long, criticizing letters from Austria, aided with secret information she received from an Austrian diplomat, Comte de Mercy-Argenteau, who was keeping a close eye on the queen. These stresses from her mother and the French people, as well as the lack of support and connection she had with her husband, Louis XVI, were believed to have led Marie

Antoinette to spend even more money on her true passions: clothing, hairstyles, shoes, makeup, gambling, and entertainment.

That would explain the biting letters from her mother that upset Marie Antoinette so much. Apparently there actually *was* someone spying on her, though it wasn't Adelaide! But whatever happened to Adelaide?

Princess Marie Adelaide of France was the favorite daughter of King Louis XV. She was exceptionally intelligent, musically gifted, and an accomplished equestrian. However, she was also extremely proud and felt as though she should not marry anyone below her royal social standing. As a result, she never married at all. On Oct. 6, 1789, Princess Adelaide and her family were forced to flee after Versailles was attacked. She lived the remainder of her life in exile and died of natural causes at the age of sixty-seven, the last survivor of her parents and siblings.

Louise couldn't help but smile. She didn't know Stella that well, but this woman sounded like she definitely matched her in the spirited-attitude department. Then her mind switched gears, as she knew she needed to keep reading what she was already aware of even if it was hard. She typed in "Marie Antoinette, French Revolution, guillotine."

THE ROYAL FAMILY WAS ARRESTED FOLLOWING A FAILED ATTEMPT TO ESCAPE PARIS, AND MARIE ANTOINETTE WAS IMPRISONED AND PUT ON TRIAL FOR CRIMES AGAINST THE STATE. HER GUILTY FATE WAS ALL BUT ASSURED, AND THE TRIAL ITSELF WAS A MERE FORMALITY. SHE HAD NO CHANCE OF PROVING HER INNOCENCE. ON OCT. 16, 1793, THE ALMOST UNRECOGNIZABLE QUEEN WAS PARADED THROUGH THE STREETS OF PARIS, HER HAIR SHORN, WEARING AN UNADORNED ANGELIC WHITE DRESS. AT THIRTY-SEVEN YEARS OLD, SHE WAS LED TO THE GUILLOTINE AND KILLED IN FRONT OF AN ANGRY MOB OF PEOPLE.

Louise knew that the revolution was necessary and that the people could not live under the horrific poverty anymore, but she still couldn't get out of her head the image of a laughing teenage girl trying on dresses and playing with her puppy. She wished things could have been different, but it was impossible. She next searched for Gabrielle de Polignac to find if a similar fate befell the queen's trusted companion. After the adventure she just had, this information felt a lot more personal.

THE BEAUTIFUL YOLANDE MARTINE GABRIELLE DE POLASTRON, DUCHESSE DE POLIGNAC, WAS PART OF THE QUEEN'S INNERMOST CIRCLE AND MARIE ANTOINETTE'S CLOSEST COMPANION. SHE LIVED IN AN APARTMENT AT THE PALACE OF VERSAILLES FOR FOURTEEN YEARS. MUCH TO HER DESPAIR, THE DUCHESSE DE POLIGNAC WAS ORDERED FOR HER OWN PROTECTION TO LEAVE THE SIDE OF MARIE ANTOINETTE AND GO INTO HIDING WITH HER FAMILY IN SWITZERLAND AFTER THE STORMING OF THE BASTILLE ON JULY 14, 1789. GABRI-ELLE NEVER RECOVERED FROM THIS SEPARATION, AND SHE FELL INTO A DEEP DEPRESSION, SICK WITH WORRY OVER THE FATE OF HER BEST FRIEND. ONCE SHE HEARD THE DEVASTATING NEWS OF MARIE ANTOINETTE'S DEATH, HER ALREADY FRAGILE HEALTH DETERIORATED, AND SHE HERSELF DIED SOON AFTER. IT WAS REPORTED THAT SHE DIED OF A BROKEN HEART.

Louise stifled a sob. Seventh-grade history books were written in such factual terms, and she was now starting to see the human side of things. How would she have handled Marie Antoinette's responsibilities at fourteen years old? She'd like to think she'd be more understanding and empathetic than the dauphine, but really, who knew, when you were torn from your family and all that is familiar at such a young age? Then to be forced to marry a strange man you had never even met before, all while someone was constantly there with a new dress or a freshly baked madeleine to distract you from what was really happening outside the gilded palace gates...

Louise was beginning to accept that maybe she couldn't control what happened hundreds of years ago, but she could try to make up for her own recent behavior in this century. She opened the drawer of her bedside table, compelled to say sorry to her parents for being angry when they told her they couldn't afford to send her on the school trip because her dad had lost his job. Her monogrammed stationery was tucked underneath the sketchbook she kept in the nightstand, and her eyes widened when she saw the last drawing she had made the other morning. The robin's egg blue dress she had dreamed about was sketched out in simple colored pencil on the top page, and it looked almost exactly like the one she had tried on in the store and was now hanging in her walk-in closet. The same one that had whisked her away to Versailles.

From under the sketchbook, Louise pulled out an invitation for the next Fashionista Sale, which Glenda must have cleverly tucked into the bindle with her blue dress when she wasn't looking. Louise unfolded the thick piece of yellow paper.

There was a smaller, folded sheet of pale lemon-colored parchment tucked inside the thick envelope, stamped with the iconic bloodred seal, that she reread with a renewed excitement.

Dearest Louise,

What you and your fellow Fashionistas share is very special. We have picked every one of you because you have an understanding of fashion, of history, and, most important, of the inextricable connection between the two. You have your friends, you have your family, and soon you will have your fellow Fashionistas. We hope you continue to learn from the past, embrace the present, and dress each day as though you have a date with destiny. Because, darling, as you should know better than anyone, you never know where the day will take you. . . .

Kiss kiss,
Marla and Glenda

Louise smiled, realizing she was now officially part of a special group of like-minded Fashionistas. In a way, it was exactly what she had always hoped for, and she couldn't wait to meet the other girls who were also on this fabulously adventurous path with her. She hastily slammed the drawer and headed downstairs to apologize to her parents in person.

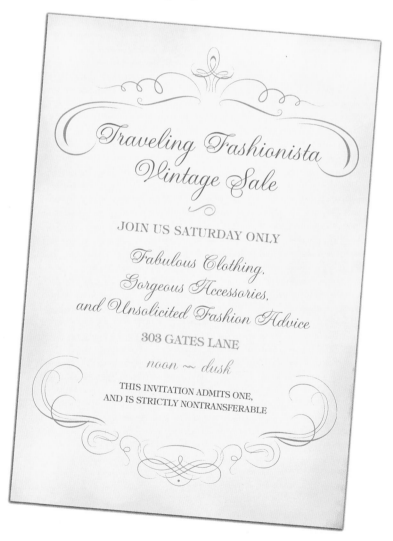

Traveling Fashionista
Vintage Sale

JOIN US SATURDAY ONLY

Fabulous Clothing,
Gorgeous Accessories,
and Unsolicited Fashion Advice

303 GATES LANE

noon ~ dusk

THIS INVITATION ADMITS ONE,
AND IS STRICTLY NONTRANSFERABLE

CHAPTER 35

The following Saturday night, Louise walked into Brooke's thirteenth birthday party with the practiced air of an actress or aristocrat who was used to making a sweeping grand entrance. She felt like she was starting to carry a little bit of her past experiences with her. After attending a ten-course dinner on the *Titanic* and a formal gala at the palace of Versailles, somehow a festive night at the Pattersons didn't seem quite as intimidating. She was still a little nervous in anticipation of seeing Todd again, but in a good, excited way.

Earlier that afternoon, Louise and Brooke had decorated the basement with silver streamers and hanging cardboard stars covered in aluminum foil. A silver disco ball Brooke's parents had rented now spun from the ceiling, its mirrors casting a million little sparkly reflections around the dimly lit rec room. Playing in the background was the party playlist they'd made on Brooke's iPhone, mostly fun dance music but with a few slow songs thrown in there.

Louise had decided against wearing the magnificent blue dress, as the thought of squeezing her swimmer shoulders back into that formfitting gown was infinitely less appealing. She didn't want to be fainting into the punch bowl, and Brooke had made it clear that by fancy-dress theme, she didn't mean eighteenth-century costume party. Together they'd picked out a less dramatic but still pretty pale lavender fitted, A-line lace dress, and Louise had half pulled back her flat-ironed hair, which was fairly frizz-free for now, as long as no one sweated on her. She had spritzed herself with her mom's Chanel No. 5; the sophisticated, floral French perfume was her only secret little reminder of the adventure she had just come from.

Todd was hanging out with a group of guys by the Ping-Pong table, his navy-and-white-striped tie loosely knotted around his untucked blue polo shirt, his baggy khaki pants still barely staying up around his plaid boxers. The skater version of fancy dress. He was talking to his best friend, Matt Waters, but waved at Louise and smiled, seeming to be genuinely happy to see her. It looked as though he was trying to say something to her across the room just as someone turned up the Strokes on the Bose speakers.

"*What?*" Louise mouthed. She was about to walk over to

them when Brooke stopped her, grabbing her arm from behind. Brooke looked gorgeous, donning a BCBG gold-sequined cocktail dress and matching-but-not-too-matchy strappy gold shoes. Her blonde hair was pulled up in a high ponytail. Thanks to her MAC bronzer, she literally glowed.

"I want to introduce you to my cousin!" she exclaimed, grabbing her by the hand. "Louise, meet Peter. His family just moved here from Boston." Louise looked up and felt a flighty sensation. Something about this guy's wavy brown hair and defined cheekbones was eerily familiar. "I thought you two would get along." Brooke pointed at his charcoal gray three-piece suit and jokingly pulled out an old-fashioned watch from his vest pocket. "Do they even make these any-more?" she asked, shaking her head.

"I don't think so," he replied, quickly tucking the tarnished watch away. "It's just something I've picked up on my travels."

"Hi," Louise stuttered, immediately forgetting her newfound confidence. She nervously twirled a wisp of flatironed hair around her index finger. "That watch is awesome. I love antiques."

"Believe me, I told him already," Brooke interjected. "You guys will have a lot of stuff to talk about. Old stuff. Peter's going to be in eighth grade at Fairview. I'm sure you'll have plenty of time to chat."

"Yeah, I start classes on Monday, so it's cool that I get to meet some people before," he said, looking at Louise intently with his green-flecked, coffee brown eyes. "It's hard to drop in somewhere and have to figure out everything for yourself."

"Come on, I want to introduce you to a few more peeps," Brooke ordered.

"All the best people, I'm sure, knowing my cousin." Peter jokingly slung his arm around Brooke and grinned at Louise over his shoulder, revealing a dimple in his left cheek.

"I guess I'll see you there," she said, her knees slightly shaking as they walked away. Peter had the exact same cute dimpled smile as her eighteenth-century French gardener crush, Pierre. *Was this real?*

"See me where?" Louise spun around, startled to see Todd standing behind her with a goofy smile on his face and carrying two red plastic cups.

"Nowhere." Louise blushed, embarrassed.

"That's too bad," he said jokingly. "Lemonade?" Todd offered her one of the cups.

"Sure, thanks," she accepted, taking a large gulp. She happily noted that Tiff was nowhere in sight.

"Hey, I've been wanting to talk to you. I think I've figured out a way for you to come to Paris. I can bring a huge suitcase, poke airholes…"

Louise laughed. "It's okay. I'm sure I'll get there at some point. Besides, I'm pretty happy to stay home for a bit. I feel like I haven't been around in a while."

"Just sayin'. Or we could go out for french fries one night. Same difference, right?" He gave her a playful punch on the arm before heading back to the table for another round of Ping-Pong.

"Thanks for the offer..." she trailed off, wondering if that was Todd's mumbled way of asking her on an actual date. Left standing alone with her cup of lemonade, Louise searched the crowded room for Peter, but he must have already left? She guessed she'd have to wait until Monday to see exactly *how* much they really did have in common. Something nervously told her it might be a lot.

CHAPTER 36

Louise couldn't sleep. Her potential french-fry date with Todd was overshadowed by the weird feeling of déjà vu she experienced after meeting Brooke's cousin Peter. She also still couldn't shake the horrific images of Marie Antoinette and the royal family that she had read about while researching on her computer.

She climbed out of bed and snuck into her closet, not wanting to wake her parents—her mother was an extremely light sleeper. Her hands went for the fastest and easiest connection to her childhood comfort zone; she tugged her mother's battered steamer trunk, with its UK flag sticker still plastered over the left side, out of the corner, making a loud scraping sound on the hardwood floor. Louise held her breath, but the house was still and quiet as she noiselessly opened the heavy lid. She pulled out her most-loved Barbie, which was wrapped discreetly in white tissue paper and dressed in a pale pink frilly ball gown. It had a short blonde punk-rock haircut, courtesy of Louise going overboard with her mother's gardening shears. Punk Rock Barbie was unfortunately missing one pink plastic shoe. She reached deeper in the trunk to find the lost high heel and instead brushed her hand on something cold and metal beneath some thin, crumply paper.

Louise carefully pulled out a long, tarnished gold chain and sharply sucked in her breath. The charm suspended from the thick links was an oval-framed picture of a black poodle. It was the same charm that Marla and Glenda both wore! Why was this necklace hidden in her mother's old luggage?

She began yanking out the Malibu Barbies, Kens, tissue paper, Barbie tennis rackets, until everything was in a pile next to her. The bottom of the trunk was lined with a piece of brown butcher paper that seemed to be tearing at the seams. Her mother would undoubtedly kill her, but Louise ripped off the lining, utterly convinced she would find something—she wasn't sure what—on the other side. She sighed, disappointed to discover it was just the inside of a bare case, but then her finger glossed over a small black-and-white photograph of her mother stuck to the back of the brown paper.

A teenage Mrs. Lambert was dressed in a long, old-fashioned white dress layered with scalloped lace trim and carrying a parasol. She was smiling at the camera, and around her neck was most definitely the poodle necklace Louise now

had in her hands. But her mother would never wear a dress like that! She couldn't stand it whenever Louise bought anything vintage. Louise squinted at the image. It looked as though a horse-drawn carriage was coming down the street in the background of the faded photograph. Didn't they have cars long before her mother was growing up?

"Louise, what are you doing awake at this hour? What was that noise?" Louise was startled by the sound of her mother's concerned voice calling from outside her bedroom door.

Her mind flashed back to Versailles when Stella asked her, "Isn't it in your family, too?"

Then her stomach dropped. There was a reason she was chosen after all. Stella was right. It *was* in her blood. The decision was probably made long before her first thrift-store purchase. Louise was destined to be a Fashionista. And she was about to find out exactly what that meant.

ACKNOWLEDGMENTS

Thank you to Cindy Eagan and her fabulous and brilliant team at Poppy, particularly Alison Impey, Pam Gruber, Lisa Moraleda, Mara Lander, and Christine Ma for working all their behind-the-scenes magic. Eternal thanks to my agent, Elisabeth Weed, and the lovely Stephanie Sun at Weed Literary. Unending gratitude to my parents for never missing a swim meet or book signing. It means the world to me. Thank you to Olatz Schnabel for providing me with the most inspiring writer's room I could have hoped for, and Gill Connon for sharing her passion and technical expertise of vintage fashion so generously with me. Big thank you to Adele Josovitz for being my first reader and unofficial regional school publicist. Thank you to Topaz Adizes for his support, encouragement, and magical book trailer. Thanks to Lucinda Blumenfeld for her tireless, creative work on this book and Justin Troust at Second Sight for creating an amazing website, www.timetravelingfashionista.com, where all the Fashionistas can connect. Special thanks to David Swanson, a great friend and an exceptional editor. *Merci beaucoup* to my grandma for being the best research assistant ever—France would not have been nearly as fun or delicious without you!

And thank you most importantly to all the Fashionista fans whose inspiring and encouraging letters and e-mails have kept me writing even when I wanted to go vintage shopping. This book would not exist without you! xoxo

NOT READY TO LEAVE YOUR TIME-TRAVEL ADVENTURE BEHIND?

Read on for more information about
France's most infamous queen,
Marie Antoinette, and the French Revolution.

TIME LINE

Marie Antoinette is born
Maria Antonia Josepha
Joanna at Hofburg Palace
in Vienna, Austria.

NOVEMBER 1755

**Marie Antoinette
officially becomes
queen of France.**
King Louis XVI
gives her Petit
Trianon, a chateau
on the grounds of
the Palace of
Versailles.

1774

1770
Fourteen-year-old
**Marie Antoinette
marries Louis XVI
of France.**

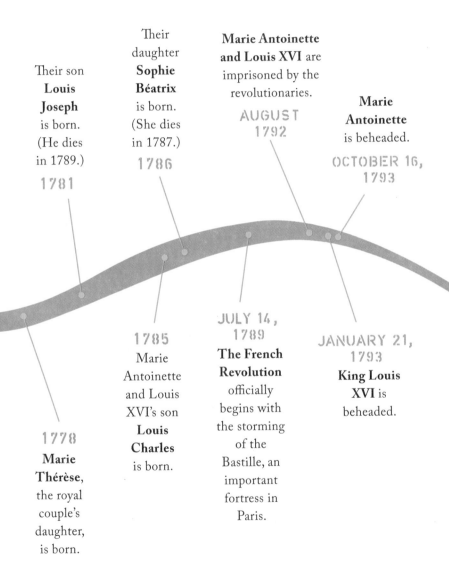

Their son
Louis Joseph is born. (He dies in 1789.)
1781

Their daughter **Sophie Béatrix** is born. (She dies in 1787.)
1786

Marie Antoinette and Louis XVI are imprisoned by the revolutionaries.
AUGUST 1792

Marie Antoinette is beheaded.
OCTOBER 16, 1793

1778
Marie Thérèse, the royal couple's daughter, is born.

1785
Marie Antoinette and Louis XVI's son **Louis Charles** is born.

JULY 14, 1789
The French Revolution officially begins with the storming of the Bastille, an important fortress in Paris.

JANUARY 21, 1793
King Louis XVI is beheaded.

The author and her grandmother
just outside the gates of the Palace of Versailles

Bianca Turetsky

Check out these resources to learn more and experience eighteenth-century France for yourself!

BOOKS:

Queen of Fashion: What Marie Antoinette Wore to the Revolution, by Caroline Weber

Marie Antoinette: The Journey, by Antonia Fraser

Shopping for Vintage: The Definitive Guide to Fashion, by Funmi Odulate

MOVIES:

Marie Antoinette, directed by Sophia Coppola (Sony Pictures Home Entertainment, 2007), DVD.

Marie Antoinette, directed by David Grubin (PBS, 2006), DVD.

Marie Antoinette: The Scapegoat Queen (Arts Magic, 2006), DVD.

WEBSITES*:

"Marie Antoinette and the French Revolution: Timeline," PBS, http://www.pbs.org/marieantoinette/timeline/index.html.

The Costumer's Guide to Movie Costumes, http://www.costumersguide.com.

Versailles and More, http://blog.catherinedelors.com.

Victoria and Albert Museum, http://www.vam.ac.uk.

Palace of Versailles, http://en.chateauversailles.fr/homepage.

*Websites accurate as of date of publication

WHAT IF A BEAUTIFUL DRESS COULD TAKE YOU BACK IN TIME?

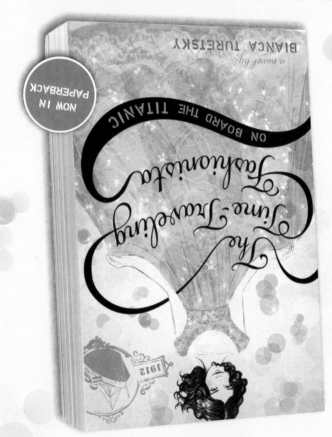

When Louise Lambert receives a mysterious invitation to a traveling vintage fashion sale, she discovers that beautiful dresses can *transport you* to a whole new era....

In Louise's first time-traveling adventure, she becomes a movie starlet on board a luxury cruise ship. Louise is living the high life until she discovers the boat's name: the *Titanic*.

POPPY

www.lb-kids.com